Mountain Spirits

Mesmerizing stories
And
Legends of Unusual Events

Rita Arnold

White Dog Books

ISBN# 978-0-9842351-6-2

Library of Congress Catalogue

Cover design by Ron D'Allessandris

Printed in the United States of America

This book is written for families who enjoy a great story.

The names and specific locations have been changed (the counties and states are correct) at the request of the people who shared their stories. If you think you know the people or locations, please respect their privacy.

Any resemblance to any person, family, or existing building is purely a coincidence. Each story was shared by a person whose family had experienced the events.

The interesting discovery in writing the following stories is how many counties share the same story; a lover's leap, a phantom train, strange happenings in an old country church cemetery, and unusual sounds in a building.

Every town, hamlet, valley has a story. Believing the stories is not important, enjoying the stories and keeping the traditions alive is vital.

Enjoy.

Ghosts of Darke County
Ghosts of Darke County II
Ghosts of Darke County III
Ghosts of Darke County IV
The Ghosts among Us
The Ghosts of Western Ohio
Stubborn Spirits

Dedication

To everyone who has enjoyed my previous books and encouraged me to continue writing.

A Special Thank You

I want to thank my publisher and editor, Cathy Pearson for the assistance and encouragement in the publishing of this book. Without her, this book would not be possible.

Table of Contents

1.   Good-Bye My Love

During book signings, I have the privilege of speaking with many whose personal history has a story of its own. Such is the case with this one. The family asked that the exact location and their names remain anonymous, but they were excited about sharing their interesting and true story.

Before the Civil War, Darke County was largely farm land with several small towns and hamlets scattered throughout the countryside. Smaller communities had their own general stores, a blacksmith shop, grain and or saw mill, and if they were really lucky they, a town doctor. Larger towns had all these plus more diverse businesses like dress makers, carpenters and, of course, the necessary undertaker.

Greenville was one of the larger towns in the county and had just about every business anyone could want. Commerce was clustered in the center of these communities with homes surrounding the business community. As is common today, successful business owners built the larger houses on the more spacious lots along a quiet street in prestigious neighborhoods.

Employees lived in the smaller homes either rented or owned, but usually on busier streets that were near their places of work.

John was a teller for the town's largest bank. He and his wife of over twenty five years enjoyed the hustle and bustle of living just a couple of blocks from main streets. They loved to sit together on the front porch in the evenings and watch the people and wagons drive past in a constant stream. People they knew would stop and visit. Such was the nature of the small town they loved.

John and Isabel were very active in their church. Hardly a week went by without their volunteering at the church to help with a community meal or attending an important meeting pertaining to improving the town.

"The busier I am, the younger I feel!" was John's constant refrain.

John and Isabel Baker had purchased the town lot next to them and turned it into a large garden with space for some flowers. Not only did they love tending it together, but it also gave Isabel a well-stocked cupboard which she used to establish herself as one of the best cooks in the county. In fact, friends often suggested that she should open a restaurant so that everyone could savor her tasty meals.

The couple was in love from the minute that they met at church many years before. As they watched the world go by from their front porch, their conversation often turned to their blessings.

"How lucky we are, John," Isabel would say. "You have a good job and we've got our health, our faith, and each other."

"You're so right, Isabel," he reply. "Life couldn't be any better for us than it already is."

John always walked the eight blocks to work, rain or shine, content to be in the middle of their growing community. But one evening, he noticed how tired he was on his way home. He shrugged off the fatigue as the result of a long day and thought nothing more about it. However, as the weeks passed, neither John nor Isabel could ignore that this daily ritual caused an increasing shortness of breath, leaving him exhausted by the time he reached home.

"Honestly, John, your clothes are hanging on you. With my cooking, you shouldn't be losing weight," she said. "Maybe you should see the doctor."

"Now, Isabel, why waste the Doc's time and our hard earned money? I'm sure my fatigue will pass," he replied.

But it didn't pass, nor did his wife quit her nagging. John finally gave in and walked the short distance to see the town's physician.

"Truthfully, John, I can't find the reason for your feeling so tired," the doctor said after examining his friend of many years. "It will probably pass. But to ease Isabel's mind, it might be a good idea to take a few days off from work and rest around the house. Have her feed you from that great garden of yours and you should be as good as new."

"Okay, Doc. But I think my wife is worrying about nothing," John said and ambled home. But Isabel's best efforts in the kitchen could not entice John to eat. His appetite was nonexistent and he became more and more tired and lethargic. Soon, he started complaining of a pain in his abdomen which quickly became unbearable.

After a few days, the doctor was summoned to the Baker's house for John and was shocked by what he saw.

"I'm deeply sorry, Isabel, I don't think there's anything I can do," he said as he patted her arm. Pulling some medicine from his bag, he continued, "Give him this whenever he complains of pain and don't worry about how much. It will help to keep him comfortable. I'm not exactly sure why, but I've been at this business long enough to know when a man's nearing the end of his life. That's what is happening to John. I'll check back in a couple of days. Call me sooner if you need me."

The Baker's world shrunk to their second floor bedroom. Isabel sat in a wooden straight-back chair next to John's bed, tightly holding his hand. Often John asked to have the window open so he could hear the outdoors sounds that he'd always loved of the bustling activity on the street; the birds chirping in the nearby shade trees, and the wagon's rolling by while the fresh air gently blew the curtains. This is how Isabel spent her time; day after long day.

Then on Friday evening, John woke and turned his face to his wife. "Isabel," he whispered in a raspy voice, "I hear it; I hear the death wagon a-comin'."

"No John," she cried, "That can't be! It can't come for you!" The tears flowed down her cheeks as she shook her head in denial of the inevitable.

"Yes, dear," he consoled her. "I'm sure of it."

His wife wanted to scream that he could not go, she wouldn't let him go, she needed him and she was scared to live without him. The tears soon became loud sobs and she tightened her grip on John's hand until she was afraid that his hand would break. Isabel sobbed uncontrollably, repeating over and over, "John, don't go, I love you so much, don't leave me, please don't leave me."

Slowly and softly John took his final breath. Uncounted minutes passed before Isabel released his hand and pulled the covers up to his shoulders. She could not bear to cover his face; the face that she'd awakened to every morning for all of her married life.

Numbed by her pain, Isabel sat quietly beside her husband's still body, tears racing down her cheeks. Finally, the sounds of the street reached her, too. Faintly at first and then louder and louder, she heard the sounds of horses' hooves and the creek of wagon wheels coming closer and closer. She crossed to the second story window and looked down into the street. The wagon had stopped in front of their small house. While she watched, the front door opened. John emerged onto the porch in his Sunday clothes and favorite dress hat and headed for the wagon. When he reached the wagon, John slowly turned, looked up at Isabel, and smiled. He tipped his hat to her and climbed aboard.

Isabel waved back to her husband and sadly watched as the wagon moved down the street. She slowly turned from the window and once again saw the body of her beloved John in the bed that they had shared for so many years. The reality of his death wiped away the recent memory of his smile.

She crossed the room, walked down the stairs and out of the front door to make her way to the doctor's office and tell him of John's passing.

The Baker's house still stands in Greenville. On a quiet night, the current residents enjoy sitting on the porch at night just like John and Isabel had so long ago. When the traffic thins out late at night, they tell of hearing the sound of a horse drawn carriage slowly making its way down the street. The sound seems to stop in front of their house, soon replaced by the whinny of horses and the inpatient stomping of their hooves. The clatter of the front door opening and, then, closing is also heard, but the door never moves. After a few minutes, the sound of the moving wagon starts again and quietly fades down the street.

Those that hear the wagon's sound describe a feeling of profound sadness, and, sometimes, the sounds of crying from the second story of the house despite that fact that the room is empty.

Occasionally, heavy footsteps are heard coming down the stairway, followed by the gentle movement of air as if someone had walked past. No one is seen!

When the air has quieted again, the silence of the night returns and peace once again descends.

2.   Step by Step

The following is a story that has been told generation after generation. I have heard other similar stories in various locations from Kentucky to Tennessee but this is my favorite version. It was shared with me by a family living in southern Sevier County, Tennessee.

In the 1840's settlers worked hard just to survive in the wilderness of the 'Land of the Blue Smoke;' now known as the Smoky Mountains. Fortunately for the settlers, this area provided plenty of game for food and furs that played an essential part in both survival and commerce for its people. Since actual currency was scarce, furs were used to trade for goods in place of coin or paper money.

Scavenging the woods for plants was also common to supplement the household diet as well as the vegetables provided from the settler's own garden- grown produce. The wives often took their children to hunt for a honey tree, wild berries, and herbs for seasoning and healing, and any greens that could be cooked. This may sound like an easy and enjoyable task with the children but it could be dangerous.

In the Land of the Blue Smoke, the weather can change quickly and become unexpectedly threatening, even to the most accurate weather observer. Anyone who has hiked in these mountains knows that a person must be vigilant of these weather changes. The constant danger of a sudden drastic shift in the weather is the backdrop of our story.

~

During an unseasonably warm November day, Sara decided to take the three youngest of her eight children with her to look for any late season greens or nuts that she could use around the house or in trade. They had walked this trail up the mountain several times that summer and in years past. The children enjoyed the adventure and Sara always marveled at the wonders of nature around her.

This area of southern Sevier County, Tennessee is now part of the Smoky Mountains National Park, but in the 1840's it was a wilderness being settled by immigrants looking to escape the crowded east coast of the new country. The soil was great for raising crops, and the grass grew abundantly for grazing cattle. Wild game was plentiful for supplementing a family's food and the forest's lumber made the dream of building a sturdy cabin and barn possible through hard work. Sara's family, and other industrious homesteaders, had created a small settlement just southwest of Townsend by using whatever was available to them.

Nestled in one of the fertile valleys was Sara's small one room log cabin, facing south to take advantage of the sun. A couple of small windows and the cabin's door were on the southern wall with a stone fireplace across the room on the northern wall. The front porch that ran the length of the cabin had wooden benches under each window. Sara and her husband, Joseph, worked hard to make the cabin warm and safe for their children.

Behind the house sat a corral and a crudely built barn for the livestock. Here the family kept a few pigs, cows, and chickens. A large garden was located behind the house. Sara took great pride in the vegetables and herbs that she grew but was frugal enough to only plant what she could not find growing in the wild.

As Sara and her three youngest children hiked up the meandering trail, she was constantly on the look out for anything usable as well as wild animals that could threaten them. The children were excellent about staying where their mother could either see them or be within shouting distance. Sara and her brood reveled in the gentle breezes and warm sun of this atypical fall day. She knew that winter would soon be upon them and wanted to enjoy the last vestiges of autumn.

A few short miles from home, she paused to look out over the valley below from her favorite spot on the familiar trail. As always, she looked at the beauty of nature and realized how much she loved these mountains. Her eight year old boy stood beside her for awhile before tugging at her sleeve and saying, "I need to be excused." Sara pointed to a large shrub and told David to come right back to her. She could see the other two children gathering nuts and greens near by, so she turned back for one more view of the valley below, basking in the feel of the sun on her face.

Sara was not usually one given to daydreaming and standing idle. But today was different. She wanted just one more look at the splendor around her before the harsh winter settled over her home. Perhaps the coming snow explained the creeping melancholy that quietly engulfed her.

She was startled from her quiet musing when she realized that she was standing in a chilly shade caused by the sun being obscured behind the dark, ominous clouds. Sara silently berated herself for woolgathering and not paying attention to the sky and the children.

The air had turned cold; so cold that she started to shiver! The breeze had become a strong wind quickly changing the weather and suddenly threatening her family's safety. She knew that a storm would soon be upon them and they needed to head for home immediately!

Two of the children were already coming toward her, shivering with the cold, but young David was no where to be found! Sara and the children called and called for him with no response. The temperature grew steadily more frigid with a bone chilling rain announcing the storm's arrival. Sara was torn between continuing to look for David and seeing the other children safely home.

The kids made the decision for her. They insisted on continuing the search while always keeping each other in sight, but David was not to be found. As the wind howled the youngsters became so scared that they began to whimper. They wanted to find their brother but they also wanted to go home. Sara did her best to remain calm but the fear seizing her heart nearly made it beat out of her chest.

When the rain turned to sleet with the wind blowing it sideways, Sara knew that they must find shelter immediately. As they started down the now treacherous path, they were met by their father coming up the trail with lanterns and coats for everyone.

Sara threw her arms around Joseph and sobbed, "David is lost! We've looked and looked but haven't found him. We've all got to go back for him"

"Sara, you and the kids are half frozen. Take them home and I'll find the boy. Go, now, I was afraid I'd lost all of you."

A couple hours later Joseph staggered through the front door. He was soaked from the pounding rain and shaking from the cold winds. His lips were blue, his hat was frozen, and the lantern nearly out of oil. Sara helped him to the fireplace, wrapped blankets around him and tried to warm him gradually. The oldest boy, Mark, was sent to the nearby neighbors to tell them what had happened.

Soon several neighbors had arrived at their cabin to offer their help in the search for David. By now Joseph had thawed out enough to talk with the men about how best to search for the boy. Some wives had come with their husbands and were busy trying to comfort Sara and the children. The women made warm tea and coffee for everyone crowded into the tiny cabin while the men filled their lanterns, bundled again in their winter coats, and soon left the cabin in teams of two or three.

"Fire a shot in the air when the boy is found," yelled one of the men. No one wanted to say "*if* the boy was found."

The sleet had now turned to a heavy, thick snow. The blowing and drifting blizzard was a major concern for the searchers. The violent storm worsened by the minute, unleashing its full fury on the mountain. The quest quickly became difficult and dangerous, but no one hesitated. Everyone knew that it could have just as easily been someone in their family who was missing. In fact, in such a small community, they felt part of a bigger extended clan that depended on each other for their very survival.

Shortly after the men had been swallowed by the storm, the local physician knocked on the cabin's door. Doc had a reputation for being the best tracker and hunter in the valley. He was also known for his strong religious beliefs. After a brief prayer at the cabin for everyone's safe return, Doc put on his glasses, secured his hat with a scarf and placed a hand gun on his hip.

"Don't worry, Sara. I'll catch up with one of the teams. With God's help, we'll find ..." His last words were engulfed by the wailing wind as he disappeared into the white-out of the blizzard.

Doc was, in fact, not a classically trained physician. He owned the local mercantile where he stocked everything from fabric, to tools, to herbs, and various medicines. These 'medicines' were mainly flavored liquids with pretty names and a high alcohol content. Doc had an excellent reputation for dispensing sound medical advice and was considered an expert at safely treating ailments and injuries. The town's people felt that a trained physician could do no better than Doc at treating the problems that arose in the small community.

Another interesting facet to Doc was the fact that he also functioned as the town's preacher. Settlers from miles around came into town to hear him preach on Sunday. His loud baritone voice preached the evils of sin and gave the congregation what he thought was the key to eternal life. He joked with his parishioners that he could marry them, deliver their children and bury them.

"With God's help, I am the whole package!" he laughed. He rounded out that package by providing the music at the harvest celebration by fiddling the night away for the annual barn dance.

Doc plowed through snow over his knees without spotting the other searchers. When he reached the location that Sara had told him was her 'viewing spot,' he started walking in circles. With each completed turn, he increased the circle circumference by three feet, always marking the area so as not to miss a possible hiding hole.

He often had to stop and wipe the moisture from his glasses. After the third time around the circle, Doc paused to clean his glasses again. When he put them back on he saw them: Footprints! *Barefoot* footprints! Small child size footprints!

No sooner had he seen them than the wind blew snow into the prints and instantly they were gone. Doc had noted the direction of the prints and pushed through the drifts with renewed energy. He prayed that he had not imagined the tiny footprints because he felt compelled to follow the direction they had indicated.

Time passed but no more prints appeared. Doc stopped to clear his glasses of snow again and said a short prayer.

"Were they real, God? Please, give me a sign. Lead me to the boy:" Then he saw them again. Footprints! *Barefoot* footprints! Small child size footprints!

Within seconds the wind again covered these prints with snow making them invisible. With determination and gratitude, Doc plowed forward in the direction that the tiny footprints indicated.

"Let him be alive, God. Give us a miracle." A miracle it would be for one so small to have survived, but Doc was a believer.

After several minutes of walking, Doc noticed something tucked against a large boulder. He wondered if it was an animal trying to protect itself from the cold, strong wind and blowing mountain snow. Then a sudden, gentle swirling wind came towards him, blew away some of the snow flurries and he saw a tiny patch of fabric. "David. DAVID!" Shouting the boy's name and stumbling in the deep snow, Doc raced towards the boy.

He gently brushed the snow away from the still body of the small boy. Immediately, his heart plummeted. The boy's lips were blue, his face ashen, and his extremities were stiff and cold. Ice had formed on the child's hair and eyelashes.

David was curled into a little ball, as if trying to protect himself from the weather. Doc just starred at the boy for a few seconds, too cold to cry and too stunned to move. He had found the boy but there was no miracle today. Young David was dead.

Refusing to leave the body, Doc lifted the boy and held him against his warm chest beneath the coarse wool of his sweater. He re-buttoned his coat around David as tightly as possible. Doc then fired a shot into the air per the agreement, picked up his lantern and slowly started walking down the trail toward the cabin. He plodded along slowly to prevent a fall. The closer to he came to the cabin, the more difficult his steps became. Doc was tired and the bundle he was carrying was growing heavier with each step. On he walked, step after weary step.

He cradled the precious bundle tightly to his chest. If only David had been found sooner. If only.

How would he tell the family that little David was dead? During his many years in medical practice, Doc had often delivered the sad news about a loved one's passing but this particular time it would more difficult. David was his nephew. Doc had delivered the boy.

Oblivious to the numbing cold, Doc paused a few feet away from the cabin's door. He saw a warm glow from the lanterns on the porch with the windows glowing from the fireplace inside. Doc knew that the news he was about to deliver would forever change that family, but prolonging the horrible facts would make them no better. "Bad news is best told just straight up," Doc reminded himself.

Doc pounded on the cabin's door and a couple of ladies rushed to help him. They pulled off his frozen hat and gloves, and heavy, snow covered coat. Then they noticed the expression on his face and they instantly stopped moving, many collapsing into tears.

Without saying a word Doc walked to one of the small beds in the corner of the cabin and gently, respectfully, laid his precious bundle on the mattress. Reaching for a blanket to cover the body, he heard a soft sigh as he slowly pulled the cover to the boys' shoulders. Gazing sorrowfully at David's tiny body lying so still, Doc tried to think of something comforting to say; something meaningful and special. How could he possibly ease the pain of losing a child?

"Help me God," he mumbled with his eyes locked on the motionless boy. Then he exclaimed, "Wait a minute! What did I just see?" Doc could not move. He starred at the tiny body, tightly closed his eyes and then looked again.

Had the blanket moved? He held his breath and waited, his eyes glued to the boys' chest. Ever so slightly the blanket moved up and down on David's tiny body. Finally, he allowed his gave to travel to David's face. His lips were no longer blue and his eyelashes moved gently against the returning pink of his cheeks.

"My, God! He's alive! David's alive!"

Shouts of joy erupted with tears of relief and pure joy. The men slapped one another on the back as they returned, forgetting their despair and frozen limbs. The women hugged each other and the children became their noisy selves again as the gloom that had enveloped them melted as easily as the snow on their father's boots. The celebration wound down and the volunteers gathered their coats and lanterns and headed towards their own cabins, with the wonder and amazement of what had just occurred still floating through their minds. Each adult clung tightly to a child's hand not wanting a replay of what had just occurred.

Doc lingered a bit longer in the cabin. "When he wakes up, give him some warm broth and keep his in bed for a couple of days. He should be just fine," he told Sara. Still having a hard time believing what had happened, Doc decided to check the boy over one more time before he left for his own cabin. That's when he noticed it! "Dear God!" he exclaimed.

David had shoes on! High button black shoes on both feet! The footprints Doc had clearly seen were barefoot: clear tracks with indentations from each toe! He remembered that his nephew never went barefoot. He wore shoes at all times. Doc checked David's feet one more time. The feet appeared to be the same size as the barefoot footprints in the snow that led Doc to find David but the feet on this boy were encased in sodden shoes.

Doc fell to his knees beside David's bed and gave a prayer of thanks for the boy that had been named for him. Sara thought that it was David's guardian angel that led Doc to her son; Doc David thought it was God himself.

To this day when people stop at the same viewing spot that Sara enjoyed all those years ago and a sudden snow storm develops; barefoot child-size footprints appear. They materialize even if no children are near the area and lead people back to the path and down the mountain to safety. The tiny footprints with indentations for each toe last only long enough for those in danger to find their way and then quickly vanish with the wind.

Is someone or something on this mountain protecting the hikers? A spirit? A ghost? A tiny guardian angel?

3.   The Dance Caller

This story takes place in one of the hollers not far from the Daniel Boone National Forest in Kentucky.   One of my co-workers tells of her experience as a teen-ager.

Eastern Kentucky has some of the most beautiful scenery in the country; the beginnings of the Appalachian Mountains, hidden valleys, coal trains rumbling along the tracks, and clear mountain streams. Mountain families are passionate about their land and heritage and have lived here for generation after generation.

In 1840 Thomas and Ann had traveled west into the wilderness from "civilized" Virginia.   Advertisements had promised cheap land with plenty of wild game for hunting. They said that the forests were so thick that a squirrel could walk for miles in the trees and never touch the ground! And the soil…the soil was reported to be so fertile that all a man needed to do was to throw the seeds on the ground and a bountiful crop would result. Of course, they failed to describe how hard life in unsettled territory could be. Though difficult,

Thomas and Ann were the first generation of a family whose roots were to run deep in those hills.

The one luxury item that Ann insisted on bringing for the long wagon trip west was her precious violin. She loved music as much as she loved her family and church. Ann could neither read nor write and had never seen a piece of sheet music in her life. But, if someone could hum or whistle a tune she could duplicate the song on her violin and have it committed to memory after playing it just one time. Folks marveled at her talent and would sit for hours listening to her perform.

This love of music was handed down from Ann to her son George who lived on the family's farm in Jackson County, Kentucky, in the early 1900's. Though he never learned to play the violin, claiming that his fingers were too clumsy for such a fragile instrument, he had the most beautiful tenor voice ever heard in the mountains. He sang at church in a full voice or while just doing his chores at home.

George knew that music would never provide a living for him and Clara, so he learned to be an excellent farmer, just like Thomas has been. Even in the early 1900's life in the mountains was not easy. Farmers like George were still plowing the fields with work horses and tending the corn and bean fields by walking the rows and manually pulling the weeds. Removing rocks was a constant chore also done by hand with the help of a strong back.

Electricity and telephones were not in every house. Usually the local general store had the only phone for miles around. Most of the people living in the hollers still used oil lanterns for light and horse drawn buggies for travel to town to visit neighbors on a Sunday afternoon.

George and Clara worked hard to make a life in the beautiful but difficult land of their parents. So did their ten children who were required to attend school, worship on Sunday at the community's church and help on the farm.

However, life was not all work for the mountain people. Communities played baseball against each other and farmers turned the harvesting of crops into social events by helping each other with the wives bringing plenty of food to feed the workers. The Fourth of July celebrations were always big, all day affairs. But the best recreation came four or five times a year in the form of a barn dance.

George and Clara always attended the dances. George grew up at the dances listening to his mother play her fiddle (that's mountain lingo for "violin") and, of course, dancing with the pretty girls. In fact, George and Clara met at a barn dance shortly after Clara and her family moved to Kentucky.

Over the years George became fascinated by the dance callers. He loved the rhythm of the caller's instructions to the dancers and the snappy patter that they used to entertain the folks. While doing his chores and thinking that he was all alone, George's mother often heard him practicing a 'call' he had memorized at the recent barn dance. "Do-se-do and gents you know, once and a half and let her go."

One night at a dance, an unsuspecting George was invited on the stage to 'call' one dance. He had no time to be nervous and stepped right up front. In the half talking/half singing style of a veteran caller he guided the happy dancers through their paces. When the dance was finished, the crowd showed their approval with prolonged applause. George was hooked. In a couple of years, George became the favorite caller in that holler and he was only eighteen years old! His signature beginning for every dance was "Howdy, y'all! Let's dance!"

A near-by community with their own favorite son heard about young George and challenged him to a dance calling contest. Word of the contest spread through both hollers and the excitement built as the big evening neared. The barn was filled to over flowing with people dancing to the dueling callers. When the evening was over, the exhausted revelers proclaimed George to be the undisputed winner.

Since George continued to support his family by farming the old homestead, he never charged a fee for calling. At every dance he set a quart size mason jar on the front right corner of the stage. There was never a cost for the dances so people dropped a token of their appreciation into the jar only if they could afford to. George never counted the money. After each dance, he just handed the jar to his smiling wife. Over the years George continued to entertain the folks in the eastern hills of Kentucky while his family proudly cheered him on.

In the 1930's hard times hit the entire country. Life in the hills grew even more difficult and families had to work together just to survive. Gasoline was in short supply, crop prices hit rock bottom and land values sank to an all-time low. Still, people continued to scratch out a living from the land by raising what they needed or bartering with their neighbors for things they couldn't produce themselves.

Barn dances were not held as often but the occasional dance gave a much needed diversion from the back-breaking work. George was still the most popular caller and was always eager to do his best so everyone could have an evening of fun.

As the 30's waned, the prospect of a dance caller's competition with entrants from four different communities made the mountains of Eastern Kentucky buzz with excitement. The best caller from each holler was invited and, of course, George was to represent his home town. As the contest date approached, people talked of nothing else.

The big Saturday night soon arrived. Mountain folks came from miles around, bringing their entire families. Many brought tents with plans to spend the night camping while others would stay with friends or relatives. Wagons were parked everywhere and the horses were turned out in a nearby pasture for the event.

The barn quickly filled to bursting, so, many people had to be satisfied to hear the music as it drifted out of the barn. No one complained. They were all excited at the possibility of their caller being acclaimed to be the best.

Four chairs were placed to the left of the stage. As the eight o'clock start time approached, the dancers realized that only three chairs were filled. George was still absent, but everyone knew that he had to be there somewhere. He would never miss an event like this.

The enormous crowd was growing restless, so the emcee announced that the competition would begin with the three who were there and George, when he showed up, would be the last caller. As the first contestant finished his dance, folks suddenly noticed that George was sitting in one of the chairs. Now, the excitement really began to build.

After the second and third man finished, George stepped up to the microphone, quietly looked at the audience and said, "Howdy, ya'll! Let's dance!" The people went wild! George's melodic tenor voice rang out, calling out "Do-si the lady, ladies do and gents you know, it's right by right by wrong you go." And on it went.

When the dancing and clapping stopped, the emcee called for quiet and the voting began. When the final raised hand was counted, he announced,

"Tonight's winner is George, y'all!"

George received a beautiful certificate, hand-drawn by a local artist and a fancy hat band for the western hat he always wore while calling a dance. In his usual modest way, George thanked the crowd for their votes and the gifts. All four of the competitors called a couple more dances and then it was time for everyone to call it a night.

The next day people noticed that George and Clara were not in church, which was very unusual. So, that afternoon the pastor went to check on them. Clara answered the knock on her door with tears in her eyes. Clara told him that last night when George was hitching up the wagon to travel to the contest, the horse spooked, bucked and kicked George in the head. He was dazed so Clara helped him back to the house to lay down for a while. George went to sleep and never woke up. Clara found him dead when she checked on him later that evening. His beautiful tenor voice would be silenced forever.

The pastor could tell that Clara was still in shock and understood why she hadn't gone for help. But everyone had seen George at the dance on Saturday night! He'd called several dances and won the contest! They'd given him the certificate and hat band.

The mystery was the talk of the hills for months. Neighbors from far and wide watched as George was laid to rest in the family cemetery next to his parents on their beloved homestead, but it made no sense. They had heard him call those dances.

Months later Clara brought herself to clean out the closet that she and George had shared for years. There on the top shelf was the certificate that George had won and the fancy new hat band! Could that crazy talk have been true? Maybe George had given voice to one final dance.

~

On a warm sunny afternoon in 1955, Lizzie, her favorite cousin and their mothers were strolling slowly along the dusty dirt road toward the general store to pick up some supplies. By now, life in the hills was a bit easier, and the teenagers were talking about boys and clothes as their moms were engrossed in their own conversation about family matters and the upcoming harvest season.

Suddenly, the girls stopped. "Shhh, y'all," the girls called with their finger against their lips.

"What's wrong, girls?" one mother answered

"Do you hear that?" Lizzie whispered. "I think I hear George practicing."

To this day, folks who walk down the now paved old country road in Jackson County, claim to hear a clear tenor voice call out.

"Howdy, y'all! Let's dance!"

4.   T'aint Funny

A friend of mine told me the following story.   Though she changed the names and was vague about the exact location, she got a big kick out of telling the tale.

The Wilson's moved into the old farm house in 1982. The house was surrounded by twenty acres of rolling pastures, three creeks flowing through the property, and the gently rolling foothills of the Appalachians.   What a great place to raise their children.

This old home was built around 1850.   The original cabin on this homestead was erected in the early 1800's and was located a ways south of the current house.   This house sits atop a hill with the front porch overlooking the Ohio River. Generations have enjoyed watching the barges travel the river or the occasional steam boat still carrying vacationers on cruises, or, just gazing at the spectacular view across the Ohio River toward the lush hills of Northern Kentucky.

Not long after the Wilson's moved into the 'new home,' they started hearing strange noises. At first the parents thought is was their twelve year old son, Scot, who loved to play tricks on people. Scot denied being involved but the prankster secretly wished that he had thought up some of these "way cool tricks."

Scot was an amateur magician who constantly practiced his 'illusions,' with his parent's encouragement. He prowled through the local library looking for books on magic tricks. Scot always had a deck of cards handy and proved to be very good doing the fancy shuffles that his idols used. He spent hours reading about the great Houdini, but his parents limited how much they allowed him to imitate Houdini's dangerous tricks.

From the middle of June to the end of August, eerie things began to occur. The original wooden first floor would creak during the afternoon as if someone was walking from the front door to the kitchen and across to the back stairway. Then, footsteps went up the stairway with each step punctuated by a thud. The door to the upstairs bedroom on the left would slam open followed by the door to the right of the hallway being kicked open, followed by a few seconds of unsettling silence. The ominous quiet is then shattered by the sound of a gun- shot.

Within minutes, the sound of furniture overturning, doors slamming shut, and muffled voices are heard. When the commotion dies down, footsteps rapidly exit the house through the front door.

Later in the evening, the sound of dripping water, as if a faucet was not completely turned off, is heard in the living room, followed by labored breathing and soft groaning near the north wall. At first, the Wilson's thought Scot was playing tricks. But at the end of July, Scot was at 4-H camp when the next episode occurred. They decided it was high time to do some serious research on the history of their house.

After spending hours reading old newspapers and all the recorded history they could locate, some very interesting facts emerged. Life along the Ohio River could be dangerous in the 1800's. River pirates used to cruise up and down the river looking for homes and businesses to raid. During one daytime invasion of the Wilson's old home, tragedy resulted. Four scraggly men barged through the front door demanding food and valuables. While shouting and vandalizing the house, one of the pirates fired a shot into the ceiling, unknowingly killing a man upstairs. He collapsed with a loud thump that reverberated through the dwelling.

Blood immediately started to "drip-drip-drip" through the floor boards leaving a huge red stain on the parlor floor below. The family cleaned the surface and readied the house for the man's funeral. As was the custom in that day, the body was prepared by the family (called lying out) and placed in the parlor. Relatives took turns sitting with the body until the start of the funeral, since custom dictated that the deceased not be left alone.

A year later, the sounds of a loud thump and the drip-drip-dripping sound was again heard in that room. Soon a large red area collected once more on the parlor's wooden floor.

Years passed and a different family lived in the house. Their teenage son loved to play practical jokes. He reveled in the house's reputation for ghostly sounds and unexplainable sights.

The boy took his turn sitting up with his uncle as he lay dying of heart problems. His bed had been moved into the parlor because it was not only his favorite room but was also convenient for the family to care for him. This particular night there were to be four other people sitting with his nephew and the boy just could not resist this opportunity for a grand practical joke.

During the day, the boy discreetly hid a jar of red berry juice and a large sand bag upstairs over the room where his uncle lay. He attached a string to the bag and ran it through the floor to the place where the boy would be sitting that night.

As the evening progressed, the boy told stories of the strange sounds and sights that he had witnessed in and around the house. With the wind blowing outside just enough to rattle the windows and thick clouds hiding the moon, the boy delighted in watching his companions become more and more nervous as the night wore on.

An edgy silence settled over the group. Only the ticking of the wall clock and the labored breathing of the dying man were heard, creating a perfectly spooky backdrop for the tales of the "haunted house" that the boy related.

The tension had become palpable when he pulled on the string causing the sand bag to thump on the upstairs floor and the jar to tip over. The red juice began to drip-drip-drip through the floor boards into the sick room. Screaming with terror, the visitors tipped over their chairs as they pushed each other out of the way to race from the room! One even jumped through the open window. The others hit the door at the same time, wedging themselves in the frame like a scene from *The Three Stooges.*

The sick uncle instantly jumped up from his death bed, his eyes big as saucers, and yelled louder than anyone. He ran right behind them as fast as his long skinny legs would carry him, wearing nothing but a sheet that flapped revealingly in the wind! The shock of seeing his dying uncle run from the house caused the young boy to faint.

No one stopped sprinting until they arrived at the closest neighbors' house, situated about a mile away. It took several minutes before anyone could calm down enough to talk. One lady fainted as she crossed the threshold. A tee-totaling man demanded a glass of 'shine, which he chugged down, followed by another, leaving him babbling the rest of the night. Most astonishing was the sight of a dying man standing in the middle of the cabin, wrapped only in a sheet. He was shaking like a leaf from head to toe as he pointed a trembling finger in the direction of his house.

A couple of hours later, when everyone had calmed down enough to talk about what had transpired, the neighbors went over to the house to investigate. Carrying a rifle, the man and his son carefully entered the house only to find the boy sitting at the table, drinking coffee and grinning from ear to ear.

The neighbor sternly wagged his finger at the boy as he lectured him about the potential dangers of practical jokes that went too far. He turned his back to the delinquent several times in disgust to the boy's way of thinking. The real reason for the gesture was to cover the laughter that threatened to erupt at the ridiculous sight of the nearly naked neighbor standing with only a bed sheet for clothes in his living room.

The boy never played a practical joke again in his life and, happily, in spite of the dire wake they were conducting, the uncle lived for many more years!

Upon learning the fascinating history of their house, the Wilson's knew what had to be done. They would preserve the house, "hauntings" and all. Not only did they ignore the red area that appeared from time to time and the drip-drip-drip that preceded it, they committed the house's strange history to pamphlets which they shared with anyone who visited.

Were they historians, or had the legacy of practical jokes been bequeathed to another generation of owners?

5. Grandma's Flowers

Many years ago an acquaintance told me this story that had been passed down in her family. She did not know if the following was based on fact or fiction but the story is interesting. The names and the location have been changed per her request.

Johnny drove south down I-75, with his blue convertible top down, heading for Atlanta and his new position as a stock broker with the largest firm in the south. His hard work had paid off and this new job meant a tremendous increase in pay and status. Johnny was on top of the world.

His Granny was so proud of him. On her own, she had raised him from a young boy, sacrificing her needs for his education. Johnny wrote to her weekly and called at least once a month. Sadly, he always had a reason why he could not return home for a visit; he was working long hours to get ahead, vacationing with his associates and making valuable contacts or spending the holidays with his friends at their upscale east coast mansions. With each disappointment, Granny said that she understood. She never let on how unhappy she was and prayed that Johnny was not ashamed of his roots.

After working for five years in Boston, this promotion to a regional manager based in Atlanta was just one more step in Johnny's climb up the corporate ladder. He knew this new job was more befitting to his Ivy League education. His goal was to work in New York City at the headquarters and he would let nothing – absolutely nothing - stand in his way.

For a brief moment Johnny thought about how far he had come from the 'holler' where he'd grown up. He had worked hard at developing an east coast accent and losing his Kentucky drawl. He wasn't a country boy any more – no sir! He was Ivy League and part of the East Coast establishment.

Without thinking Johnny turned east off of I-75 just south of Lexington heading toward eastern Kentucky. It was a gorgeous summer day, and Johnny was enjoying the feel of the warm sun and the wind. After driving southeast for two or three hours, Johnny roused himself from daydreaming about his new life of endless possibilities and realized where he was.

He was way off the interstate. He had no time for side trips. What had he been thinking?

****

Johnny was born in Eastern Kentucky in the area that is now Johnson County, near the Kentucky/West Virginia state line. This is the beginning of the Appalachian Mountains. There's plenty of flat land for farming, but also thickly wooded hills that are a breeding ground for wildlife. The run off from the creeks in the hills keep the lower streams constantly flowing with clear, cold water and plentiful fish. Since the 1800's, coal has provided a livelihood for the residents and for outside speculators. Coal has been black gold for years.

In the 1954, Johnny arrived as the first born of Big John and Ruby who lived in one of the many hollers in this region of Kentucky. Life was hard but strong family roots kept folks tied to the state. For many, the '50s were a time of hot cars, drive-ins, traveling and enjoying things like the birth of rock n' roll. But in this part of Kentucky, life was all about scratching out a living by working in the mines, running moon shine, or giving up the hollers to seek a better life.

Big John worked in the mines just like his Daddy and Granddaddy before him. And, just like his relatives, Big John was tragically killed in a mine cave-in leaving behind a young wife and a five year old son.

Six months after Big John died, Ruby died giving birth to her second child. Her daughter did not survive either. Johnny soon went to live with his widowed Grandmother who owned a farm just ten miles to the west.

From the very beginning Granny could tell that Johnny was special. He read everything that he could get his hands on and remembered everything! Granny was amazed that Johnny could retain the smallest of details from the layout of the garden in previous years to the exact amount and variety of seeds that grew best in their soil.

She accidentally discovered that he had amazing math ability. One fall day, she was trying to decide if the time was right for selling the corn crop or if she could wait for a better price. Johnny looked at the rate per bushel and then at their meager savings. His calculations enabled them to acquire more money than she'd expected.   From that time on, she never hesitated to seek Johnny's opinion about their finances.

Granny made sure that Johnny attended school.   She cleaned houses for a couple of the wealthy families in the area and worked her own farm. She sold or bartered her eggs at the local store along with extra vegetables from her garden to pay for Johnny's education.   Fortunately, he loved school and worked all the odd jobs he could find to help his Grandmother. Johnny's studies paid off. He won a scholarship to Dartmouth a week after his graduation. Granny was so proud of her boy. She never dreamt that it would be years before he returned.

Johnny fit immediately into his new environment and made friends easily. All of his collegiate acquaintances were from well-established eastern families and freely discussed their pedigrees. Johnny, however, was always vague about his background and birthplace, telling his pals that he grew up 'south of Lexington,' omitting that he'd actually grown up *way* south east of Lexington in a small holler.

Johnny quickly fell in love with the high society life style; the nice clothes and frequent parties where no one seemed to have a care in the world. Making money and having a good time absorbed them completely. This was just fine for a fella who'd been reared in poverty and back-breaking work.

It seemed that all his college classmates had traveled the world. Johnny's knowledge of exotic, far-away places came from reading books or looking at National Geographic magazines at the tiny library in his school back home.

Upon graduation, Johnny secured a job with a prestigious New York firm's Boston branch. Now this was more like it – a fancy office, great restaurants, the shows and the women - glamour everywhere! His boss advised Johnny to put in a couple of years in Boston and then transfer to Atlanta for a couple more. Finally, if he worked hard and was lucky, he'd move to headquarters in New York City and into a vice presidency job. He was truly on the fast track of realizing his dream. Look out, Wall Street! Johnny from the holler was on his way!

So, why was he slowly driving on an old country highway that twisted and turned around the hills and old homesteads? He was being propelled through the countryside as if he had no control over what was happening. Every turn brought back memories of his childhood; small farms houses with a covered front porch holding wooden rocking chairs, clothes drying on the lines behind them, vegetable gardens and chickens running care-free around the barnyard.

After rounding a curve, Johnny noticed an old, run-down building badly in need of paint. In front of the dilapidated building, a sign read: "General Store." Johnny stopped the car, got out and stretched and stood there for a few minutes just taking it all in. Then, he ambled toward the front door.

A young boy about ten year's old sat on the end of the porch, softly crying. The boy's clothes were dirty, torn and full of holes. No one else was around.

Johnny approached the boy and asked, "What's the matter, young man?"

"I want to buy some flowers for Mama. She loves flowers but all I have is a dollar. Today's her birthday and I promised her I would always bring her some flowers on her birthday," the young boy said as he choked back a sob.

It broke Johnny's heart. He remembered being that age, wanting to buy something for his Granny but never having enough money. But it was different now. Johnny bought some flowers and walked back to the boy on the porch.

"Here you go, kid. Happy Birthday to your Mom."

"Thanks, Mister. Thanks so much," he said, a huge smile splitting his face before the raced from the store.

Johnny watched him run and then, slapped his forehead. Today was also his Granny's birthday. He re-entered the store and asked the clerk to send her some flowers. After signing a small card, he got back into his car with a satisfied smile on his face and headed toward the interstate, his thoughts once again centered on the next step in Atlanta on his climb to the top.

At the edge of town, an old cemetery stood whose markers leaned every which way. Even so, the grass was well trimmed and the trees throughout the graves were healthy and lush. The old benches scattered around had all been freshly painted. Johnny glanced at it and quickly stopped the car because of what he saw.

On the far side of the graveyard was the young boy from the store, kneeling near a headstone as he placed the flowers on the grave.

Johnny parked the car, walked to the boy and placed his hand on his shoulder.

The boy was smiling, but tears threatened to erupt again. "Mama died three years ago but I always bring flowers for her birthday. But Daddy said we didn't have the money for flowers this year and I didn't know what to do until you came along. I know Mama's happy now, Mister. They're real pretty."

The lump in Johnny's throat put him in peril of tears of his own. He patted the boy's shoulder one more time and shoved his hands in his pockets. Looking down at the ground, Johnny turned and slowly walked back to the car.

For a couple of minutes, he just sat there staring blankly out of the windshield. He took off his designer sunglasses, rubbed his face and eyes with a shaking hand and took a deep breath. He knew what he wanted to do before another day or another minute passed.

He turned the car around and headed back to the store. "Have you sent those flowers yet?" he asked.

"Not yet," the clerk replied.

"I think I'll deliver them, myself," he said.

She smiled as she handed the bouquet across the counter. "You have a good visit with your Grandma."

Shortly after that, Johnny presented the flowers to his smiling Granny, intending to stay for a couple of hours and then be on his way. She hugged him tightly with her frail arms and grinned through happy tears. He couldn't get over how much older she looked. This strong woman moved more slowly and couldn't stand as straight as he remembered. But one thing hadn't changed: she never complained about a thing.

The visit stretched into several days with Johnny easily falling into the routine of his old life. With Granny supervising from her rocking chair on the porch, he worked on the farm buildings: painting a couple of doors, nailing some of the side boards, and oiling the equipment that was starting to rust.

One evening they were sitting on the porch in the cool evening breeze sipping iced tea and chatting. "Say, I stopped at the old store when I first got here," he said. He told her about the boy and his trip to graveyard. "Who is he, anyway?"

"Why, that's young Billy" she smiled. "Don't you remember that old yarn about Billy and the flowers? Well, son, that's who you met. Guess he just decided to help me out. See, another tale that these hills believe is that if someone you love hasn't been home in a long while, if you just pray every night for a solid month, then your missing kin will show up again." Johnny laughed at the story and retired for the night.

The next day Johnny drove back to the general store and talked with the same clerk who had originally sold him the flowers. "I've sold a lot of flowers to folks for Billy over the years; most of them to people who grew up around here and moved away," she winked.

"See, Billy came from a family that was poor even by our standards. His Mama caught a fever one spring and died a few days later. Billy's heart was broken. He visited his mother's grave every Sunday right after church. He picked wild flowers for her when he could, and begged his Dad for money for better ones. Six months to the day after she passed, Billy was thrown from their old horse, cracked his head and died on the spot. They laid him to rest next to his Mama."

Johnny just stared at her. "Years passed before anyone thought any more about Billy," she continued. "Then one day a man who'd been gone for several years came home and found a boy crying on our porch. That was the beginning. I guess young Billy just wants to keep families together. Roots go deep around here. Just look at you and your Granny."

Lots of folks have "seen" Billy when they come home to visit the family. And many of them extend their vacations and end up eventually moving back. Johnny did just that. In fact, he never did return to his fast paced, high society life. Johnny found work at the local bank and eventually became its' president.

He married that store clerk. Granny lived for several more years on the family farm with their help. Johnny discovered that he had never enjoyed his life more than there among the hills of his birth. Every year on the anniversary of his return to Kentucky, they shared a meal with Granny, whose blessing always began with the same prayer: "Thank you, God, for Billy's helping us all be together again."

Mountain Spirits

6.   A Conversation

The following is a story that I read in one of the old Darke County newspapers published in the late 1800s. The exact location wasn't reported, nor its factual truth. To this day, people still discuss the old apple tree; some laughingly and others as if the story is true.

Jake, his parents and six siblings and all their families moved to the 'wildernesses' of the western territory in the early 1820's. The allure of cheap fertile land and a chance for a new beginning just could not be ignored. Some of the early settlers were leaving problems behind in the eastern territories while others just wanted to play an important role in a developing community.   Some folks just wanted the excitement of a new adventure.

Out of necessity, Jake and his wife Rebecca planted a large vegetable garden as soon as possible. This produce, along with Jake's success at hunting game, was able to help the family eat during the first winter in their new homeland. The following year, Jake was able to obtain fruit tree seedlings. Rebecca was thrilled to now be tending the apple, cherry, and walnut trees. She could hardly wait for them to mature.

As the years passed, Rebecca could be seen watering her fruit trees, staking and re-staking the trees as they grew, and constantly increasing the height of the fence that surrounded the trees. No cow, pig or wild critter was going to damage her precious trees.

Rebecca loved apples! She made apple pie, canned apples, apple cobbler, applesauce or glazed apples, but her favorite apple was the one that was plucked off the tree and eaten fresh. Nothing pleased her more.

Rebecca was widely known for her apples. She used them as currency; trading them at the local mercantile for her family necessities such as fabric, shoes and seeds. Neighbors eagerly awaited her arrival at community events because they knew her contribution to the pot luck meals would be one of her fabulous apple concoctions. Her apples were also the tangible means to express her generosity. When Rebecca knew a family had fallen on hard times, they might discover that a bushel of the fruit or half a dozen jars of canned apples had been left on their front porch.

One crisp fall afternoon, Rebecca plucked an apple from her favorite tree which sat a short distance from the dirt road near the bend in the road leading toward town. Here, Rebecca could view her garden, see her clean clothes hanging on the line behind the small cabin or enjoy a few minutes in the cool shade of the old tree's large, outstretched branches.

In private moments, she actually spoke the tree.

"Well, old friend, we're growing old together. You know, I'm going to be forty-two on my next birthday!" She said as she slid down the trunk to sit at the trees' roots. "Wish I could just linger here in the sun and breezes all day. But, I've got to get the clothes down from the line and cook supper."

She had taken one last, big bite of apple before standing when, suddenly there was a loud, ear splitting "BOOM!" and the large, hard fruit stuck in the back of her throat. She coughed and gagged and coughed but nothing would dislodge that apple bite! She grasped her throat in panic as the eyes in her reddening face widened and spilled tears of pure terror. She struggled for long, terrible moments before she silently fell to the ground on her right side, never to breathe again.

Later that day, her husband came in from working the fields. The stove was cold which meant no hot water for washing. There were still clothes hanging in the breeze, nothing to eat and no sign of his wife.

"Rebecca, where in heaven's name are you? I'm starving! Rebecca! Hey, Rebecca!" he called, but got no answer.

His frustration quickly changed to anxiety when his repeated calls went unanswered. He headed toward her beloved orchard at a run hoping to find her daydreaming beneath that big old tree. And there she was, back against its' trunk, her head using a gnarled root as a pillow.

Jake fell to his knees and gently shook her. "Honey, wake up. Didn't you hear me calling?" But her unseeing eyes just stared at him and her blue lips remained silent. He hugged her to his chest, shaking his head. "No, oh God, no. Rebecca, don't leave me. Please don't leave," he cried as he rocked back and forth, back and forth.

The sun was beginning to set as Jake gently lifted Rebecca into his arms and carried her back to their cabin. He tenderly placed her on their feather bed, touched her cheek and ran to the barn. He jumped bareback on his horse and flew the short distance to the neighbors. Still dazed, he dismounted and sat down heavily on the wood porch, his head against the cabin front.

"Jake, what brings you here?" asked his friend, George. Unable to speak, Jake looked at his friend through red-rimmed eyes and raised his hands helplessly. "Martha, get out here!"

Fearing the worst, they got Jake back on his horse and together trotted back to his friend's home. The church bell soon pealed out over the farms, alerting everyone of a death in their community. Word spread and a few hours later, local women arrived to wash and prepare the body for burial since their small town had no undertaker.

They gently closed Rebecca's eyes, but, try as they might, they could not close her mouth. That last bite of apple had lodged in such a way that it was impossible to remove. So, they finished their work and lovingly covered her with a sheet to await the wooden coffin. No one could bear seeing the remnants of her final scream frozen on her face. The next day, they arranged her body in the simple casket and buried Rebecca among her beloved apple trees.

A few years after Rebecca's passing a couple of women walked past the old orchard, reminiscing about Rebecca and her famous apple dishes. They paused at the foot of the old tree where they heard the sound of quiet crying. They circled the tree, finding no one, but the aroma of an apple pie baking overwhelmed them.

They looked at each other, neither saying a word, turned in tandem and quickly walked on to town. This episode was never mentioned to anyone. Several years passed and the ladies were part of a bunch of locals enjoying a community picnic on a gorgeous spring day. The talk soon turned into a kind of 'remember when' conversation about their friends and families.

One brave woman quietly giggled before admitting that she heard crying when she walked by Rebecca's grave near the old apple tree. That did it. One after another, the entire gathering fessed up to hearing the same sounds and being engulfed by the smell of baking apple pie. One bold soul added the most unusual tale. After the crying and aroma, he had tentatively touched the trunk of the old tree and pulled it back wet on a day that was bone dry. Of course, subsequent visitors had to test that theory. Most claimed that not only was the tree inexplicably moist, but, should you lean against its' trunk, your shirt would be wet enough to actually wring water from it.

Three theories evolved about what caused the damp tree trunk though there was no rain or dew to explain it. Some believed that they were Rebecca's tears, longing to still be near her family and beloved orchard. Others held that the old tree itself was weeping, missing Rebecca and her appreciation of the fruit it bore. The third group assumed the first two had imaginations that worked overtime.

The road is now paved. The cabin is long gone. There are just a couple of trees left standing in the old orchard. The small area around the old trees has been left idle for years and years. The wooden marker that designated the final resting place of Rebecca has either deteriorated or was removed.

Mountain Spirits

Only a few of the families that have lived nearby for generations even remember the solitary grave among the trees.

However, even the newest residents talk of the scent of apples from trees that now show only leaves. And, more than one admits to searching for the source of nearly inaudible weeping near the largest tree and the trunk that leaves your hand wet no matter what the weather.

Perhaps Rebecca still tends those trees.

7.   Thump – Thump – Thump - Thud

The following story was shared with me by a lady whose sister lives in Claiborne County, Tennessee, just south of Cumberland Gap. It's a beautiful area of mountains and lush, fertile valleys with old homes dotting the land and a fascinating history of families living there for several generations.

Kathy and her husband Michael decided after several years of living northwest of Dayton, Ohio, that it was time to move to Claiborne County. Kathy had relatives living there whom she and her husband had visited with more and more frequency as the years passed.

The visits began as stopovers on their way to Pigeon Forge, Tennessee. But with each trip, the stays became longer and longer. Michael was growing more attached to the area and yearned to leave large urban living in cold climates behind him. The final break was made with the north and Kathy and Michael moved south.

They soon found a lovely old two story brick house situated on about 50 acres on the side of a mountain. They were close to relatives yet had plenty of space for a large garden and, maybe, some grapes, and a few fruit trees to round things out. Michael also wanted to set aside about thirty acres for wildlife to live without any fear of hunters.

One sunny summer day they were walking through the twenty wooded acres when they noticed a large number of honey trees. After talking with Kathy's uncle, they decided to harvest the honey and set up a roadside stand. Being away from the crime ridden city, they took a chance on the honor system. With no one to work the stand, they set up their tables, put out the honey with a sign and hoped their neighbors would leave the money in the empty jar they'd left as a "cash register."

It worked. Soon Kathy and Michael had a growing business selling the honey, beeswax candles, and even produce from the garden when it was in season.

Kathy and Michael loved their new life. They'd even grown accustomed to the thumping noise they heard around four in the afternoon on the first Tuesday of each month. After a couple of years, they decided to research the history of the old homestead to figure out what that sound might be.

They discovered that the original owner of their property was a man named Jonah. He had no interest in farming or any other strenuous labor, but he had other skills. He was one of the few people who could read and write in the community. He knew that with families moving into the "wilderness" at such a rapid pace, a huge demand for dry goods would come with them. During the 1830's, the relative isolation of the original homestead grew quickly as did Jonah's business ventures. Folks talked about Jonah as having the "Midas Touch."

Soon Jonah had built a small cabin on his fifty acres next to the only road. He nailed a sign on the front porch post that read "JONAH'S MERCANTILE – COMING SOON." He and his two teen-aged sons took the family wagon and headed back east with his small savings and great hopes of purchasing some needed goods to sell to his new neighbors.

With the promise of returning the following year for more purchases, Jonah convinced the merchants back east to sell him goods such as shovels, gloves, plows, seeds, fabric, buttons, paint, and other products at a price that would allow him to resell them back home. Jonah hoped that his prices would be low enough for his neighbors until they started making money with their farming but high enough that he would make a handsome profit. After all, he was a businessman!

Over the years Jonah's store thrived. It quickly became the center of town. People picked up their mail at his business, purchased their needed items and traded or sold some of their farms' produce. The store was so successful that Jonah soon built a separate building fifty yards down the road from his home.

The original one room cabin was enlarged several times for his growing family. The "man with the Midas Touch" did well enough that his house now contained an open stairway to the upstairs in the front and a back stairway that lead directly into the kitchen.

Jonah loved his family, his community and his store. He loved the way his family enjoyed working with him and knew that one day his sons would take over the business. As the surrounding town grew, the citizens decided to build a structure that could house the school during the week days and the community church on Sundays. They turned to Jonah for his advice on the project and he was proud to head the campaign to raise the needed funds. As the town's most prosperous citizen, he agreed to provide the materials needed for the building at cost.

During the late 1880's, Jonah developed a fever during a severe winter. After days of careful nursing by his family and daily visits by the local doctor, Jonah became delirious from the constant high fever.

One day about four o'clock in the afternoon, his wife was dozing in the bedside chair from the exhaustion of caring for her husband and his business. Jonah stood up and wandered out of the room. In his delirium, he shuffled to the top of the stairway, lost his balance and fell to the first floor; thump – thump – thump – thud. With his neck broken, Jonah died instantly.

His family and the community were stunned! Everyone had been praying for Jonah to survive his illness. The store was closed and every person for miles around came to the funeral.

The family had a private discussion the night of the funeral and decided unanimously that Jonah would want the store to continue. The next day the store opened with the entire family working, not only for the sake of the business, but to thank their neighbors for the support they'd shown. For many years following Jonah's death, the store continued to thrive.

In 1931, the entire country was suffering from the depression and the family had no choice but to close the store. Dry goods were difficult to acquire and, besides, with few people working, there was no money to buy anything new.

Jonah's widow stayed in the area with her relatives. All the children moved away hoping to find work that was not available in their rural surroundings. The store and house were sold for a fraction of the value.

During the following years, the house had several owners. Finally Kathy and Michael arrived and fell in love with the farm and the old house. They'd even begun a small business on the site where "the man with the Midas Touch" had begun his venture so many years before.

After learning the probable cause of the thump – thump – thump – thud, Michael and Kathy developed a remodeling plan to close off that stairway, creating a small storage room on the second floor. They would still have the front stairway and maybe poor Jonah would stop falling down the stairs.

They did the work themselves and were very pleased with the finished product. They had an extra storage room upstairs and more space in the kitchen without the intruding stairway. When the remodeling was completed, they were sure that they would not hear the thumping anymore.

The first Tuesday of the following month, they made sure that they were home. In fact, they invited some of their friends to witness the results of their renovations. At 3:45 in the afternoon, a hush fell over the guests. They knew why they'd been invited and didn't want to miss a thing since some had heard the monthly thump-thump-thump-thud for themselves. Would they hear Jonah falling down the stairs or would the house's make-over silence it forever?

They all sat quietly in their chairs or stood in the kitchen. Most of them looked nervously at their watches every couple of minutes. As the minute hands moved closer and closer to four o'clock even the visitors' breathing became subdued. No one fidgeted; no one moved! The windows were open but no wind or bird song or scraping branch was heard. It seemed that even Mother Nature was holding her breath

3:59. Would Jonah fall? Or would he rest in peace? Some of the crowd was relaxed and smiling as if at a party while others were holding their breath or even complaining of lightheadedness. Almost time; almost time!

Silence...silence and then.........................THUMP - THUMP – THUMP – THUD! How could that be? The stairs had been removed!

Some people laughed nervously while others sat stone still, staring in amazement at nothing.

Kathy and Michael looked at each other and smiled. Well, why not? This was Jonah's house before it was theirs. If he'd loved it as much as they did, why would he want to leave? From that day forward, they kept a small throw rug where the base of the stairs used to be to soften Jonah's fall. Now, on the first Tuesday of each month around 4:00, they heard thump – thump – thump – bump!

"You know, Michael, I think Jonah approves of the renovations," Kathy told her husband. "Why else would he stick around to let us know that he's landing softly in the home he loved?"

Mountain Spirits

8.   Cemetery Event

This is another tale told and retold for years and years. Though the details may have been exaggerated in the telling, the woman who shared it with me swears that the events really happened to her relative.

During the years after the Civil War many men were wandering about the countryside looking for work or maybe a place to settle. Some men had developed a wander lust to see other parts of the country because of their travels during the war. For many of the former soldiers, their enlistment had forced their first adventure outside of their birthplace.

Sam was born in 1842 and raised in eastern Maryland, just south of Westminster. All eight of his close kit siblings worked together on the family grain and livestock farm. Sam often talked to his father about stories that he heard at the general store of land out west in Ohio and Kentucky. The available opportunities were so enticing that the idea of moving simply would not let go.

Some nights, Sam dreamt of the lush, fertile land just over to horizon. At other times, his ambitions turned toward owning a general store or any store for that matter, to satisfy the needs of a developing territory. He often tried to sell the family patriarch on the idea.

"Think of the possibilities, Dad. The family could make a real mark in the new territories," Sam reasoned.

"Sam, I like our life here in Maryland. Why in Heaven's Name would I want to move?" he replied.

"For the adventure!" he exclaimed, "or the chance to start a new business that would make the family's future even brighter."

"Son, my roots are here. I thought you loved our farm as much as I do. Besides, as the oldest, it would be hard to carry on without you."

"I know my responsibility, Dad. And I'm grateful for the wonderful life we have thanks to your hard work to make our family business such a success."

Though he didn't stop thinking of the West, Sam got back to work for his father and their family. Sometimes, life has a way of intervening in the best plans.

Sam's ancestors had fought proudly and with honor in the Revolutionary war, so when the Civil War began, he felt it was now his duty to enlist. He fought for the North even though some of his friends and neighbors signed on as Confederates. He did not want to see the country divided like many "secessionists" suggested. He felt strongly that it must remain united.

Sam was one of the fortunate soldiers who survived the war with no physical injuries. During the conflict, he became friends with a fellow soldier from Dayton, Ohio. Sam still wanted to visit this part of the country, and then possibly head south into Kentucky or maybe Tennessee. Sam learned that his family's farm had been a battlefield in the war and felt certain that when he did return home, his responsibilities to the family might prevent him from ever traveling again. He would be needed more now than ever.

Well, Sam made his trip to Ohio when the war came to an end. In an area northwest of Dayton, in what is now Englewood, Sam explored beautiful wooded land with streams flowing with clear water. There were already several small developments and crossroad towns, but there still remained lots of unclaimed territory.

Sam was very impressed. He decided to wander around the area for a few days and then look up his army buddy. To save money Sam camped out at night with coffee and jerky serving as his breakfast.

As the sun was setting, Sam rode along what is now called the Great Miami River and soon found a good place to set up camp. In a thick copse of trees, Sam efficiently cared for his horse and collected a stack of fire wood. About fifteen to twenty feet away was a small cemetery surrounded by a wooden split rail fence. After surviving the war, sleeping next to the dead bothered him not at all.

He ate a supper consisting of fish from the river and strong hot coffee. Sam checked his horse one more time and then lay down for the night. He wrapped himself in the white wool blanket he had found during the war and now considered his lucky charm. That blanket had covered him at Gettysburg, Shiloh and even Appomattox. He'd come to regard it as his special shield.

As usual, Sam had his pistol under the covers for protection. A couple of hours later Sam awoke to hear the slow, soft steps of a horse approaching. Without moving, he opened his eyes to watch the cemetery while straining to hear where the approaching sound originated.

He finally made out something clearly on horseback that repeatedly bent over the mount, first on one side and then the other. But he saw no head atop the gray colored coat. The horse and ghostly rider moved steadily closer to the side of the graveyard nearest to Sam. The steady "clop-clop-clop-clop became louder and louder though the rider was still indistinguishable.

When they were only about twenty feet away, Sam took action. With the pistol in his right hand and his left hand tightly clutching the white blanket wrapped around him, he slowing stood up.

When this white 'thing' rose in the mist before them, the horse reared and took off at break-neck speed, with the arms of the gray coat holding the galloping steed just to stay on the frightened horse's back. Sam watched them disappear and heard no further sounds in the silent night. Shrugging, he lay back down to get more sleep, quickly forgetting about what had just happened.

The next morning, Sam broke camp and soon met up with his army buddy who showed him his slice of the new land as they reminisced about their stint in service to the country. But Sam was restless to head back east to help his father with the war damaged farm.

"Thanks for the hospitality," Sam clasped his pal's hand, "but it's time to get back to Maryland."

"I understand," he replied. "Maybe I'll come east someday and you can return the favor."

"You're always welcome," Sam said.

Twenty years passed with only occasional letters between the friends. Then, in late spring, Sam got word that his pal was finally taking him up on the invitation he'd extended so long ago. During the two decades since they'd last talked, Sam had taken over running the family farm. Though his parents were still alive, it was Sam who'd restored the homestead and made it thrive with the help of his younger siblings. He was eager to show off his success to the friend of his youth.

Sam and his buddy had a great visit. His pal fit right in, helping with the farm chores and laughing with Sam's very large family. On the last night his stay, the friends got to reminiscing about some of the strange and often funny things that happened during their military service.

"Let me tell you about camping on the night before I made it to your place. You'll never believe what happened," Sam confided. When the tale of the ghostly rider at the cemetery was finished, his buddy burst into uncontrollable laughter.

He finally caught his breath, he said, "All these years, I thought for sure I'd seen a ghost!"

"What?" Sam said, "That was you?"

"Yeah, it was me. Earlier that day I'd been in the graveyard, tending to a relative's grave and lost a spur. On my way home from a church social, I decided to take time to look for that lost spur and thought I was about to be shot by one of the cemetery's residents!"

"Are you kidding?" Sam laughed. "I thought I'd seen a headless rider!"

"Nah, that was just me trying to bend over the horse far enough to see the ground."

"I thought you'd come to put me into the ground," and the laughter erupted again.

This story was shared by both families for generations. Both Sam, his buddy and their progeny loved boasting that they'd not only seen a ghost, but had known him personally and talked to him!

9. Young Love

Stories of young lovers are universal. Some have happy endings, some sad, and some stories are just interesting. The following story came from a lady whose family considers it a part of their history. Whether you believe the story or not, it is fascinating.

Rose once again had an apple dangling from her mouth with the stem clenched firmly between her teeth. Her right hand twisted the apple like you would a door knob. With each complete twist of the apple Rose mentally recited a letter from the alphabet. The apple always broke free of the stem on the fourth turn, the letter "D." As every young girl living in the hills of Laurel County, Kentucky, in the early 1830's knew, it meant that she would marry a man whose first name began with "D."

Sixteen year old Rose thought long and hard but knew of no boy whose first name began with the letter "D." In her teen-age logic, she surmised that she had not yet met her husband to be. Or, Heaven forbid, did it mean that she would never marry? Would he be tall or short, rich or poor, handsome or average? Rose contemplated on all of the possibilities. No matter how many times she performed the apple test, the only outcome was the letter "D."

Whenever Rose had some private time, she walked down a mountain path to the stream a short distance away. Here she could sit on one of the large rocks that lined the creek and watch the fall leaves flow gently on the clear water. It was also the perfect time to daydream of the man whose first name began with a "D."

Rose's favorite spot was situated under a huge oak tree. She loved to remove the caps from acorns, turn them upside down before placing them in the water and watch them float down stream. She pretended to be placing a boat in the water, a toy her family could not afford.

Rose picked some bright yellow dandelion blossoms along the way to her rock seat. Her apron pocket was full of acorns and the dandelions were clutched in her left hand. With her free right hand, she lowered herself onto the rock under the big oak.

Today she placed a tiny bloom into each upturned acorn cap and set them afloat on the water. She set only four tiny boats adrift because that was the number that exactly matched the number of turns on her apple.

The tiny navy floated away under her wishful gaze when suddenly she heard soft splashing coming from down-stream. Though startled, she wasn't afraid. By standing on her rock she saw a young man, probably in his late teens that she'd never seen before. He was so handsome that her breath caught in her throat.

"Hi" the fella called with a wave. "My name is David Douglas Duncan. We just moved here a few days ago from over in western Virginia. Who are you?"

It took Rose a few seconds before she could reply. The boy's name had three letters "D!" She wanted to jump for joy, but said instead, "Hi, yourself. I'm Rose."

She climbed over the stones as he made his way up the stream toward her. They talked the afternoon away and agreed to see each other at the local Baptist church on Sunday. The sun was setting as Rose hurried home to do her chores and David trotted off in the opposite direction to help his father with the evening milking.

David and Rose did see one another that Sunday and every Sunday after that. In the early spring of the following year, just like the twisting apple had foretold, they were married. They built a small cabin close to David's father so they could help with the farm that David would one day inherit.

Rose's father opposed the marriage. No one knew anything about David or his family and he was very protective of his young daughter. Remembering an old mountain superstition, he nailed an old iron horse shoe upside down on the young couple's house (exactly the opposite position that most chose.) This way, good luck might spill out and maybe Rose would come to her senses, leave this stranger and return home.

Soon, strange things did begin to happen. David's best work horse went lame, making spring plowing difficult with only one good horse. Then the plow broke and needed the blacksmith to do the repair work.

No matter how hard Rose tried, the meals were never cooked to her liking. She had been cooking ever since she could stand but for some unexplained reason, the wood stove in her cabin just wouldn't work properly. No matter what she tried, her food was terrible, though David never complained. She was really upset when her mother fixed a meal there and everything turned out great! Rose slumped in the chair with her hands over her face and said over and over, "I don't get it, I just don't get it."

Despite all the problems, David and Rose remained head-over-heels in love and Rose never even considered running back to her parents. A couple of months later Rose realized that she was pregnant with their first child. She and David were thrilled and rushed over to tell her parents. News of a first grandchild was so exciting that even Rose's father was happy enough to embrace his son-in-law for the first time.

The next day, Rose's father paid the young couple a visit.

"I've got a confession to make," he said.

"What is it, Daddy?" Rose asked.

"I didn't know anything about this boy who was stealing my daughter. When I nailed that horseshoe to your house, I put it up the wrong way so that you'd come back to your mother and me. All that bad luck you've had, it was all my fault. I brought the hammer over to take that thing down. Rose really is a good cook."

"I'll look forward to the change, Grandpa," David laughed.

Sadly, Rose had a lot of problems with her pregnancy. The baby was born early one morning. The delivery was terribly hard and Rose died in childbirth. Her father's grief was unbearable. No one could comfort the man; not his pastor, his family or his neighbors. He blamed himself for the loss of his daughter. Why had he ever nailed that cursed horseshoe to their home?

Inconsolable, he began to withdraw from life. He neglected the farm, failing to care for the crops or his livestock. He lost weight since all he would do was sit porch staring into space while barely picking at the meals his wife put in front of him. Finally, he stopped speaking at all, responding to questions with only a grunt.

One hot afternoon his wife stepped onto the porch after weeding the garden and looked closely at her husband. He was sitting in the wooden chair, same as always, with his chin against his chest as if he'd fallen asleep. Tenderly, she reached out and touched his cheek, but pulled her hand back as if it had been bitten. His skin was stone cold. Her husband had finally laid down his sadness and died.

The next day he was buried in the plot next to his daughter. The town doc said he must have died of a heart attack but everyone else knew better; he had died of a broken heart.

For quite a while after Rose's father was laid to rest, whenever someone visited his grave, they saw a single print of a horse shoe in the ground beside the headstone. Even stranger, her father's marker never stood straight. People did everything they could to realign that tombstone, but nothing worked for long. Sooner or later, the blasted thing would again lean to the left, away from his daughter's grave. In contrast, her headstone never moved or needed adjustment.

Years later the marker fell over and no one tried to fix it. It was left to lie on the ground. To this day, Rose's tombstone still stands tall. Rose never blamed her father for the strange events that she and David endured, but her Dad blamed himself. Long after departing this life, the guilt of his mistake endured.

Can a person die from guilt?

10.   The Love Letter

The following story has its origin in a love letter; yes – a love letter. It was written in the1860's as a man left his home to fight in the War Between the States. A lady told me this story a few years ago. The great granddaughter of John Thomas and his wife, May, is proud that the love letter is still in the family, being passed from generation to generation.

Growing up in a military family, John Thomas, whose family always called him by both his first and last names, dreamed of soldiering. At age sixteen he met and immediately fell in love with fourteen year old, May. Giving up his dreams of a military life, he and May eloped and left for eastern Tennessee where their ten children were born. May and John Thomas had a strong faith and a belief in hard work. They were proud that their seven boys and three girls survived infancy and became excellent workers in the store and on the farm.

John Thomas' general store specialized in hardware and lumber. As the profits increased, he expanded the store with a larger variety of items as well as adding tools and farming equipment. He stocked fabric, sewing supplies, home remedies and a few gift items, but his favorite time was spent selling the growing inventory of tools and farming equipment. He also sold or bartered for the purchase of farmland. His land holdings became quite extensive.

John Thomas was proud of his family and of his successful business. All of the children attended the local one room school and as a family they enjoyed being active in their church. If bad weather or an illness kept them home on Sunday, John Thomas led them in their own Bible study.

As the children grew they were all given chores to do around the farm and at the store. May was in her glory caring for the house, making clothes for her children, and helping her husband at the store, too, whenever she was needed.

John Thomas and May were considered a living love story throughout the county. They were often seen holding hands while walking about town or sitting in church. No one ever heard a cross word or a raised voice pass between them. The children often told their friends that they hoped to find their true love just like their parents had.

In 1861, when a rider announced that Fort Sumter was being fired upon, John Thomas knew instantly the War had begun. On hearing the news, he quickly removed his apron and rode his favorite horse at a furious pace from town straight to the porch of his log cabin. His wife, on hearing him calling her name, came running from inside, drying her hands on a towel and yelling, "What's happened? Are you hurt?"

"It's happened!" John Thomas jumped off his horse. "The war had started!"

May stood frozen in place, wringing her hands together, and already praying for their sons. To May, war was soldiers dying and families being torn apart. To John Thomas war was glory; a chance to fight for honor, justice, and their way of life. They argued all through the night with John Thomas explaining why he felt called to fight for the South and May, fearing for his life, pleading that their family needed him. They agreed to not do to anything until after church on Sunday which was only three days away.

That Sunday afternoon a large group of about one hundred men made plans to join the fight but only if John

Thomas would be in charge and lead them into battle. He was a humble man, but was proud that his friends and neighbors were willing to follow him to fight for the Southern cause and protect their way of life. They all felt the Confederacy must never die. John Thomas was soon elected to become the Colonel of the local regiment.

The day of departure arrived bright and sunny. As the men prepared to leave, many a tearful farewell could be seen throughout their community. John Thomas, like most men looking forward to the glory and suppressing the idea of death, vowed to survive the battles and come home safe and sound. He promised to write May as often as possible and pray for the well-being of her and the children daily. With flags waving and people wildly cheering, John Thomas sat proudly on his horse at the head of the regiment and led the town's men to war.

Mail service was slow before the war and even slower during the conflict. Telegraph service soon came to town and with it came a list of the local men wounded or killed in battle. Almost daily, people walked to the telegraph office to study the listings posted on the outside wall telling of the latest casualties.

Mixed emotions greeted each new list that was posted; there were sighs of relief, tears of grief or silent smiles of happiness that a loved one had not been killed or injured. Still others screamed their misery over the loss of a husband, father, brother, or son. The wretchedness of these poor souls caused even the lucky ones who, once again, did not find their loved ones' names on the list, to wrap themselves around their neighbors anguish in an attempt to console the inconsolable.

Finally, May collected a long awaited letter from John Thomas.

My Darling May,

I know that soon we will march into battle. I feel confident that the men are well trained   and will make a good showing as the proud Tennesseans they are.

I do not wish to die but I know, through my faith, that should I die, I will be waiting for you in Heaven. And there we will spend eternity - together.

May set the letter aside. This was her first letter in weeks and she wanted to read her husband's words slowly and savor them. She carefully folded the letter and placed it in the top dresser drawer to read later that night after the children were in bed. She was exhausted from carrying the responsibility of the whole family and she was nearly sick with worry about John Thomas. But she worked even harder to be positive for the children's sake. They were so stoic to pitch in with no complaints that she felt she owed them as happy a home life as she could manage.

May spent most of her days at the store, scrounging to obtain whatever goods she could find. Most products were either in very short supply or not available at all because of the war. Cash was also scarce so May learned to barter well. She also ran a tab for those who couldn't afford to pay. The thought that one of her neighbors might go hungry because the father was fighting was more than she could bear.

That night after the kids were all in their beds, May pulled the precious letter from her dresser, adjusted the lantern as she sat on the edge of her bed and devoured the words written in a hand she knew so well.

Rita Arnold

May – my love for you is endless. When I close my eyes I feel as if I can reach out and touch your warm cheek. If a man could be in two places simultaneously, that I would gladly do. I love and miss you beyond words but I also love my home state of Tennessee and our way of life. I remember all of our wonderful memories; the day we met, the day we wed, when our children were born, and most of all, you. The warm, loving looks we shared, holding your hand as we walked to church, your gentle way with the children and your constant support and encouragement in all of our endeavors. Oh, how I wish I could hold you now.

Should anything happen to me, how I would miss being with you and seeing our children grow into adulthood. I do not wish to die, but I will do my duty to fight for the Confederacy.

May put the letter to her chest and closed her eyes. She was desperately afraid for her husband. She quietly prayed and then continued to read as one tear silently slid down her cheek.

May forgive me my thoughtlessness and many faults, I never wanted to disappoint you. I always did my best for you and the children.

If I should die, I promise the last word I'll utter will be your name. I know the dead do not return to earth, but if you should feel a gentle touch on your cheek, that will be me, wanting to be with you. I will be with you always in the darkest of nights and the brightest of days. And some morning as you awaken for a new day, should you reach across the bed and feel warmth on the mattress, that will be my spirit comforting you. You will never, NEVER be alone.

Do not mourn me for long. Live your life, for we will meet again.

Your loving husband,

John Thomas

May shed no more tears. She placed the letter back in the drawer under her clothes and never read it again.

One month later May walked to the telegraph office. One of her friends embraced her in front of the list of casualties from the battle at Gettysburg. A chill ran up her spine and she forced herself to read. "Colonel John Thomas" was listed among the dead. May was stunned. She just stood there, unable to move, unable to think. Her thoughts finally returned, thinking of the grief her children must now bear. How would she tell them the news?

May knew there would be no body to bring home. John Thomas had died for what he believed in, his beloved Confederacy. He died fighting with his fellow soldiers and there he would remain.

Two days later May stood in the town cemetery with her family and the other women of the town. A marker was erected with the inscription 'John Thomas, loving husband and father.' The cemetery had recently seen too many burials of the town's young men. Hugging her children to her, they all wept in a place with far too many fresh graves.

For years after losing her husband, May and the children continued to farm their land and operate a successful general store. Ten years to the day after being notified of John Thomas' death, May passed away in her sleep. She was buried in the town cemetery next to the marker that commemorated John Thomas.

Female descendants of John Thomas and May who they lived on the family homestead often reported feeling a gentle touch on their cheek. On those occasions when their husbands weren't sleeping at home, wives told of waking to find a warm spot on the mattress beside them. Succeeding generations believed that they had not only inherited the land but also the special love that their ancestor's letter described. John Thomas and May were still touching the hearts of those they loved.

11.   Enduring Love

Several years ago two sisters shared this story about their grandparents. Their mother was in the house at the time the interesting events happened. They had never known their mother to lie therefore they felt this story was true. As one of the sisters told me, believe it or not, it's a good story. In fact, it's a very good story.

Robert and Caroline were both born in the western part of Ohio now known as Miami County. Robert's family had moved west from Maryland to start a grain farm and have the adventure of living in a developing area, often referred to as "The Wilderness." Caroline's family moved there from the coast line of what is now North Carolina to avoid the hurricanes and to open a blacksmith shop.

Robert and Caroline met the first year they attended school. As soon as Robert saw Caroline he was smitten. They had others to play with at recess and to eat lunch with under the old maple shade tree at school, but every day, going to and coming from school, they were seen walking together, sharing special looks.

Their friendship deepened as the years passed. They sat together at the church socials, danced together at the local barn dances, and spent time with each others' families.

Robbie had a deep love for his country and the opportunities available to anyone willing to work hard. He loved the farming life and dreamed of the day he could leave his schooling and be able to work full time next to his father on the family grain farm. But Robbie's Dad insisted on his son finishing his education, knowing that it would make a difference in the success of any business in the growing country.

Carrie had a natural talent for sewing. As a teenager she began to sew for neighbors and family and was soon earning money as a seamstress. Carrie never tired of sewing and took great pride in her work.

Carrie dreamt of opening a dress shop and owning her own business. Many of her classmates were rushing into marriage shortly after graduation. If she owned a dress shop then she would be in charge of her own life and income. "Could an independent woman survive in this world?" Carrie wondered.

But there was also Robbie. Carrie had so much fun with Robbie that she often forgot about the dress shop as she dreamed of a future as his wife. Then one Saturday evening, things got out of hand and the two young people spent too much time together. Within a couple of months Carrie knew which direction her future would take. She talked with Robbie after school one afternoon and the decision was made. This would be their secret.

Carrie and Robbie graduated in May and the next month they were married in the bride's home with just family members witnessing the ceremony. The in-laws spoke of the special love between the two young people and how there could not be a better match anywhere. That explained, they reasoned, why the bride was positively radiant whenever she looked at her true love. Robbie just smiled into her eyes and silently acknowledged their secret.

Robbie had already built a small house for his bride on his father's farm. Here they set up housekeeping and dreamed of a great future together. The early birth of their first child barely raised an eyebrow.

As the mid 1800's drew near, they both knew that the possibility of war was becoming more real every day. They followed the news as best they could though it was usually a few weeks or months late getting to them.

Soon a militia was formed by friends and neighbors and, after a long discussion with Carrie, Robbie signed up. A big part of Robbie's decision was pride – he did not want his buddies to think he was afraid of fighting. Most communities had a militia long before the advent of war.

In 1861 Robbie, along with his friends and neighbors, rode off to war. Robbie fought bravely at Gettysburg and Shiloh. Fortunately, he was one of the few lucky soldiers to fight in major battles and survive without injury. But the sights and sounds of war were horrific: soldiers maimed and killed, property destroyed and farms much like Robbie's were burned to bare, scorched earth.

Summer of 1865 found a war weary Robbie riding home in his dirty, torn, Union uniform. Carrie ran out to meet his horse. He dismounted and they hugged and hugged and cried and hugged some more, unable to speak from the sheer relief of the reunion.

When he found his voice at last, Robbie said, "Promise me that you will not ask me about the war. I just want to live on this farm and forget about the last four years of death and destruction." Carrie nodded her agreement and they never spoke of the war again.

Robbie and Carrie lived in their small farm house for many years, raising six children and giving thanks for everything they had. The children grew to become wonderful, responsible adults and Robbie and Carrie continued to live out their lives deeply in love.

Robbie worked every day of his life on the farm and Carrie continued to make money sewing for her neighbors. The couple did whatever they could to support themselves. No matter how old he became, Robbie went happily to work on his beloved farm. In 1910, Robbie collapsed in his corn field. When he failed to come home for his noon meal, Carrie went looking for him and found him on the ground with his favorite old hoe lying beside his body. Carrie knew immediately that Robbie, her one and only love, was gone.

Family and friends had soon gathered at Carrie's house to comfort and assist her with funeral preparations. The next day, with her children supporting her, she buried Robbie in the town cemetery. A small oaken marker, carved by Robbie's oldest son, served as the headstone of his father's grave.

When the graveside service concluded, Carrie remained standing there alone, her family a few feet away to give her privacy. She quietly whispered, "My only love, I will miss you so, but I'll be with you again one day. How glorious our reunion will be."

The family worried how Carrie would cope with so great a loss. But Carrie did just fine. She continued to earn money with the sewing she'd always enjoyed. In fact, Carrie's clothes were so popular that she could hardly keep up with the orders. She even expanded her "line" to include quilts that were so beautiful that they sold as fast as she could make them.

Carrie's youngest daughter, Barbara, came over for lunch almost daily, to check on her and to visit with her mother. They enjoyed these times with just the two of them chatting away the hours. Barbara often helped with some chore that took two people or drove her mother on her errands.

About four years after Robbie's passing, during one of her visits, Carrie declared to Barbara (the mother of the two sisters who shared this story), "I don't want anyone to wear somber, black clothes when I die. You see," she said with a smile, "I'll be with my Robbie again and that's a reason to celebrate."

One month later Carrie developed a fever and soon slipped into a coma. The family stood vigil at her bedside day and night. Barbara was sitting with Carrie one night while another daughter, Elizabeth, sat in her father's den, unable to witness her mother's deteriorating condition.

One by one, the other relatives drifted in and out of Carrie's room, standing quietly and listening to Carrie's slow, gentle breathing. Elizabeth remained sitting in her father's den, inexplicably feeling that she should remain there.

The house was quiet. A couple of cousins sat in the parlor, watching the flickering flames in the fireplace. Elizabeth, thinking she heard Carrie's door open, started to stand up from the old brown leather chair, then immediately sat down when she really took a good look at who was in front of her.

Standing at attention in his Union uniform, was her father, Robbie. He looked so young and handsome as he smiled at the daughter who looked like a younger version of his wife. With a small nod of his head, he left the den, walked through the parlor and exited the house from the front door.

Elizabeth sat there for several minutes, not sure of what had just happened. Was she dreaming or had she really seen her father? Was the stress of the long vigil driving her crazy? After taking several deep breaths, Elizabeth stood on shaky legs and slowly walked out of the den.

Elizabeth stepped into the parlor and saw big smiles on her cousins' faces. "You saw him, didn't you?"

They both nodded their heads and spoke at once. "Oh, yes!" "You, too?" "Did you see how happy he looked?" "What a huge smile he wore!"

A somber Barbara entered the room. "Mother is gone," she said. Her sister and cousins rushed to embrace her, standing silently now with their arms around each other. After a few moments, she disengaged from the hug with a smile on her face. "You know, Mom hasn't looked that happy in a long time. She was positively glowing, just like a new bride when she first sees her bridegroom."

No one in the family reports seeing the ghosts of either Robbie or Carrie, but they do talk about a feeling of happiness whenever they visit the old homestead. And, inevitably, one of the next generations retells the legend of the last time that Robbie came home for his Carrie.

Mountain Spirits

12.   Screams for Help

While selling my books at a Farmer's Market one sunny Saturday morning, a lady who was visiting from Kentucky stopped at my booth. She bought a couple of my books and then began to share some stories from her home county. Though she wasn't sure if there was any truth to the story, she sure enjoyed telling the tale!

Growing up during the Depression years was difficult for people, especially if you were living in rural Kentucky in the foothills of the Appalachians. That is the where we meet Willie and Anna Lee.

They were both born in 1915 on neighboring farms a few miles east of what is now the Renfro Valley. At that time, the area was a sparsely populated farming community since it was still years before the interstate system created more densely populated towns.

Most of the families living there during the early 1930's were just barely surviving off the land by growing their own vegetables and raising a few cows and pigs. Others had chickens for eggs and meat which put food on the table or provided a bit of income at market. They supplemented their meager food supplies with what they could shoot on the mountain, adding rabbit, squirrel, deer, wild turkey, and the rare black bear to their diet.

There was a strong sense of tradition in the hills populated by descendants of people who had settled the region years before. They handed down clothes from one child to another and repaired broken household items instead of buying new. They made what they needed for the farm instead of ordering a new piece of equipment or they loaned what they had back and forth with their neighbors. Bartering for goods was a way of life made necessary since most people had very little currency.

Willie and Anna Lee attended the same rural one room school, when possible. Both of their families wanted the children to have an education. Appalachian parents dreamed of every child graduating from high school. The problem for Willie and Anna Lee was that each was the eldest child in their families and they were often needed at home which meant that they frequently missed their studies.

Willie and Anna Lee never complained if they had to miss school. They were not happy about it because they both enjoyed their classes, but they understood if they were needed at home. Family was very important to both of them and that was just the way life was.

Going through school together and seeing each other at church on Sundays, Willie and Anna Lee developed a close friendship. They liked each other's relatives, they enjoyed country living, and were not afraid of hard work. The families celebrated birthdays and holidays together and helped each other with the butchering or canning as the seasons demanded.

Willie and Anna Lee and their siblings enjoyed hiking on the nearest mountain. Whenever the children could get some time away from their chores, they hiked up the mountain to enjoy the view, watch for wild life, hunt for berries and nuts from the walnut grove or just do nothing. Time away from the constant work was a treat for the kids.

In the days before television, computers and cell phones, outdoor adventures were the only source of entertainment. What today might be considered "getting exercise" was just fun without expense back then. Anyone growing up beside the mountain learned to enjoy walking at an early age.

Willie and Anna Lee had one favorite trail that they enjoyed every spring. With the younger children they would walk up almost to the summit and there they could enjoy the view looking out over the large boulders and watching the fast flowing stream below. The younger children were always carefully watched and warned not to go near the edge of the rocks since there was a long drop from the cliff.

One warm spring day, Willie, Anna Lee and three of the younger children were sitting on the mountain at Anna Lee's favorite spot overlooking the valley below. Anna Lee had packed a basket of apples and cookies for everyone and Willie had filled two canteens from the small stream of ice cold water. They were relishing their idleness as they ate their snacks, talked and laughed.

Suddenly, Anna Lee spotted an eagle flying overhead. He gracefully circled and circled with his wings spread wide.

His smooth flight had so captivated them that they fell silent, all eyes glued to one as they traced the magnificent creature above them.

Without thinking, Anna Lee stood up on the forbidden boulder to watch the eagle dive gracefully towards the stream, snag a fish with its talons and zoom back up and over the mountain top. It soon returned and floated toward the stream once again. Anna Lee was so engrossed that she leaned further and further over the boulder, hypnotized by the awesome patterns in the sky. She simply could not take her eyes off that eagle.

Everyone was equally mesmerized by the fishing eagle and took no notice of Anna Lee. Suddenly they heard a piercing scream! Willie yelled, "Annie!" and raced towards the boulder, catching himself at the very edge of the rock. He sprawled on the stone and crawled to the cliff's edge.

He watched in horror as she fell over the mountain side, her screams for help becoming more and more faint the further she fell. Far below, Willie could see her face down in the stream with her arms spread out at right angles and her right leg bent at an impossible angle. No one moved for a second, and then everyone began talking, screaming and crying all at once. It was pure pandemonium!

Willie knew that she could not have survived the fall and the panic of the children could cause another tragedy. Knowing he could do nothing to help Anna Lee, Willie quickly hustled all the youngsters back to their homes where their mothers consoled the hysterical kids. Willie led the fathers back to the stream for Anna Lee.

Two days later Anna Lee was buried high on the mountain that she loved. The school was closed for a few days of mourning and sadness enveloped the hills. People wanted to talk about what happened but no one knew what to say. How can you make sense out of a tragedy that claims so young a life?

Both families remained in the Renfro valley; in fact, some of the descendants live there still. Near the summit lies a single grave whose wooden marker has since been replaced by a gravestone.

People walking up the mountain often report seeing a young girl in the distance, leading the way up to the top.

When she reaches the summit, she tips her head back and watches the sky as she comes closer and closer to the edge of the cliff. Suddenly, she slips from sight, with the sound of her screams growing softer and softer as if she were falling, falling, falling for a very long way. Brave souls have crawled to the cliff's edge and looked below where the only thing they see is the rushing stream.

.

Hikers who stand by the lonely gravesite often see a solitary eagle soaring through the sky overhead, sometimes accompanied by the eerie cries for help. But the most unusual occurrence is finding a single eagle feather lying next to Anna Lee's headstone in the graveyard for one.

Mountain Spirits

13.   Scary Train Crossing

It this story true? No one can say for sure but I am sure that almost every county in the nation has a similar story that probably becomes better with each passing year. This tale takes place in Greene County, Ohio in a town that was abandoned years ago.

"Listen! The train is coming!" said Tommy. It was October in 1956 and the boys were hanging out together in the rural country of Greene County.

Homer replied, "No way! Remember, they removed the tracks a couple of years ago."

"But listen…" Tommy insisted. The boys held their breath and heard the sound of a distant train coming in their direction. Speechless, they looked at each other as the trains' approaching sounds grew louder and louder.

"Let's head for the barn," Homer finally shouted. "I heard that a tornado sounds just like a train. I don't want to get caught in a twister!" The boys turned on the spot and raced as fast as their legs would carry them back to Tommy's barn.

After a several minutes, the boys were finally able to catch their breath as they paced around and around the barn. Tommy repeatedly ran his right hand through his red hair while Homer chewed on one fingernail after another. Both boys were sweating heavily, possibly because of their mad dash, or, maybe from the sense of encountering something so unexplainable that they'd started to shake.

Tommy broke the silence. "Man, I never believed that old tale my Granny used to tell. We just heard the ghost train. Man, oh man! I still can't believe it!" They had stopped pacing and sat facing each other on hay bales.

"What are you talking about?" Homer asked.

"I'll tell you," Tommy replied, "but you've got to promise that you'll never tell anyone that we ran from the 'ghost train.'"

"Are you kidding?" Homer replied. "The guys at school would never stop laughing at us. I promise," he said as he ran a finger over his heart in the shape of a cross and raised his hand. Tommy spit on his right hand and extended it to Homer who repeated the gesture. The friends solemnly shook and Tommy began the tale.

~

Many years ago, trains ran through Greene County every two or three hours. The trains never slowed down in this part of the county since the nearest depot was about fifteen miles away to the north. During the days of trains and buggies, the only structures near the tracks were a feed mill, a tiny general store, a whitewashed church with a small cemetery behind it and a small tavern. The tavern served a locally made, but not very good beer and some food. There were also four rooms up a set of creaking stairs that rented by the night or hour, whichever made money for the owner.

One night in the late 1890's a young man and his lady friend had eaten passable meatloaf dinners at the tavern. While she sipped a lukewarm beer, he motioned to the barkeep to bring his third – or was it fourth? – glass of the home-made brew. She noticed his glance repeatedly move toward the rickety stairs that led, she could only assume, to the end of an evening she wasn't sure about.

"It's such a nice fall night," she mused. "How about we take a walk?"

"Sure, why not?" he replied, trying to hide his disappointment. "The night is young," he said as he held her chair and took her arm. He walked past the bar to pay for their meals and threw a meaningful wink at the owner who smiled and nodded.

They strolled arm and arm for a while down the dirt road that ran in front of the scattering of buildings with her date telling tall tales in an attempt to impress his date enough to get the evening back on track. She smiled and murmured encouragement as he continued to brag.

"And I can outrun any man for miles around," he boasted."

"I'm sure you can," she said as a train's horn tooted its' approach with the clatter on the tracks getting louder and louder in the dark.

"I can even outrun that train you hear," he said. "And I'll prove it. You stand here, out of the way. I'll cross that track before it can get to the end of this building," he said, handing his hat to his date.

"Don't be silly," she said as the engine's headlight bore down on them. "It's not slowing down! Stop! Stop!" she screamed, but he had broken into a dead run. She watched in horror as he launched himself, silhouetted against the dark in the train's light. Unfortunately, he'd misjudged the rails' placement in the night's gloom and tripped.

It happened so fast that the man didn't even have time to scream. The engineer, who never slowed as he moved past the few buildings, must not have seen the impetuous young man. He was in mid-air as the locomotive hit him at full speed and threw his body into the dark night on the other side of the tracks. Or did it?

The stunned woman raced back to the tavern. Between gulps of air and fainting spells she told the patrons what had happened, punctuating the story with hysterical bursts of "He's gone, he's gone, he's gone." Finally, she pointed a shaking hand toward the door and fainted a fourth time.

The tavern emptied as patrons grabbed lanterns and raced into the night but found nothing. After the sun came up the next day, several men returned to continue searching but still without results. After a few hours, the fellas walked back into the tavern to wash the dust from their throats with a beer. As he set the glasses on the bar, the owner said, "You'd think there would have been a shoe or a piece of clothing, or at least part of his body. This makes no sense."

Why was a body not found? The poor guy's lady friend was never seen again in that tavern or anywhere in the small community where everyone knew each other. Was this some kind of sick joke played on the patrons of the tavern or something more sinister? A suicide? Planned disappearance? What???

Years later, usually on an autumn night, folks swore that they'd seen a man dashing in front of a fast moving train that still clattered down tracks that had been removed. But the next day, there is no trace of a terrible accident or even footprints in the dirt where the rails had once been.

Tommy and Homer kept their promise and never mentioned what they saw that late October night to anyone. If a neighbor told them of a personal encounter with the "ghost train," the childhood friends would just smile to themselves, never confirming their own belief in the truth of a story rooted in their own experience and Granny's tall tale.

Mountain Spirits

14.   Knock – Knock

When this story was shared with me I told the gentleman that I had heard of other people facing similar situations. This story could have happened in anywhere but lucky for me this version occurred in Tennessee and I was able to hear the tale.

Back in the mid 1800's Jacob was a successful business man in Eastern Tennessee. He built a small saw mill along a strong flowing stream near a community on the main trail that ran north and south. As the territory grew, Jacob enlarged his mill and employed several men in the running of his operation. He also built a large two story log cabin to accommodate his growing family that included eleven children and his parents. There were three generations living in this household.

Jacob's wife, June, was active in the local church which he also attended. He was motivated, not by faith, but his desire to keep her happy and to be seen by others in their town. He knew it was good for business to be seen as an upstanding member of the community. Besides, an idle morning of sitting and daydreaming through the sermon was a welcome break from his labors.

Jacob loved his work and the money it provided. He also had a lucrative hobby. Among his male friends he was known as 'Mooney' for brewing a liquid drink favored among men but frowned on by their church-going wives.

June knew and disapproved of his hobby of operating a still back in the woods. They often had 'strong' words about "his hobby." She begged and begged him to stop. Jacob refused.

"I work *&#% hard to provide for all the mouths I have to feed. I deserve a bit of relaxation."

June went so far as to threaten to take the children and leave. But then, Jacob would bring home a new piece of furniture for the house or jewelry for her and June's complaints faded away.

Jacob was not about to stop having a good time with his buddies or give up the money he made from selling 'shine' to men in the nearby counties. Soon, tending the still took more and more of Jacob's time and he left running the mill in the hands of his foreman.

He enlarged the still and built a small cabin to hold the supplies needed to brew moonshine. That cabin quickly took on an atmosphere of a rowdy tavern where frequent booze-fed brawls occurred and, sometimes, feuds were born.

June continued to complain to Jacob's deaf ears. "You're neglecting your business and your family. And the whole town talks about what an embarrassment that still is to me and the whole town!"

His reply was often explosive. "Stop nagging at me, you *%#@ woman. You live very well on the money I bring home. So shut the %&#@$@ up!"

June didn't back down. "You have no business attending church like a decent person."

"Fine, I'll spend Sunday morning working at the still and being with my buddies. They understand me!" June usually ended these fights by stomping her foot loudly on the wood floor. Jacob's response was to laugh at her, making her madder, then walk out of the house and head for his still.

One evening while tending the still and drinking with his friends, Jacob tripped and fell face first into the fire. His screams of agony brought the men quickly. They pulled him from the flames and carried him home with his clothing still smoldering. Two days passed in unremitting torment before Jacob slipped into a coma and died.

A week later, June, his mother, and several other ladies from the community grabbed hatchets and axes and marched into the woods to the hated still. They proceeded to destroy everything in sight. They chopped and burned and chopped and burned until anything associated with that still was obliterated. With their mission completed, the triumphant women marched back home and never returned again to that loathsome place.

Over the years, Jacob and Junes' house had several owners. By the 1980's the old homestead was unrecognizable. White wood siding had been applied to the main dwelling and two large additions. The home now boasted gourmet kitchen, a large family room and a master bedroom suite with a bathroom to die for. Most recently all new wiring had been installed to allow for the use of computers and upscale media equipment.

Lucy and her computer programmer husband purchased the isolated house in the late 1980's. He was a solitary soul who loved living out in the country away from crowds and being surrounded by the woods and wild life that wandered around the area.

But Lucy was more of a city girl whose love of the isolation of country living only went so far. She did enjoy the beauty of the area but missed the convenience of near -by stores, neighbors and the buzz of city life.

Her refuge was reading and she dreamed that someday she would write the next great novel. Maybe living in the country would give her the inspiration and the quiet time to write.

One spring day an unusually violent storm swept through the valley. Her husband had just called to say that he would be working late, possibly though the night, on a computer upgrade for one of his customers in town. This was not unusual in his line of work.

By late afternoon Lucy had finished the house cleaning for the day and fresh baked cookies were cooling in the pantry. She decided to have a cup of hot black coffee and sit down in the family room to watch the storm brewing outside. About thirty minutes later, the power went out and the phones went dead.

She wasn't worried. Power surges frequently happened and she knew the lights would be back on before too long. As she fetched the usual flashlights and candles, Lucy heard the thunder abate and the storm ease to a soft, steady rain.

Knock – Knock – Knock

What was that? Startled, Lucy sloshed a bit of coffee onto the floor. She'd never heard anything like that before. Sure the house creaked like old bones but that wasn't unusual. "Don't all old houses creak and moan?" she said aloud to reassure herself.

Knock – Knock – Knock

"That's upstairs in the bedroom," she said, continuing her one sided conversation. Then she fell silent. What if someone had broken into the house? She had never, never been afraid before, but now she was starting to get nervous.

Sitting quietly, barely breathing for fear of making a sound she debated what to do.

Knock – Knock – Knock

Tip toeing into the kitchen, Lucy grabbed the first thing she saw – a can of pop! Placing it in her right hand and carrying a flashlight in her left she slowly climbed the stairs to the bedroom. When she reached the second floor landing she paused and took some slow deep breaths, trying to slow the pounding in her chest.

She was starting to shake but wanted to find that source of the noise.

Knock – Knock – Knock

It sounded like someone was in the attic! Standing frozen to the floor, she thought about what to do. The attic was filled with old family treasures, broken furniture, and just some junk they did not want to part with. Someone was up there. Why? These were their memories. These were their treasures! The thought of such a betrayal, a violation made her mad!

And being mad was a good thing. It spurred Lucy into action. With a new determination, she put her fears aside and decided to confront the intruder. "No body - no *&%$#@ body was going to invade this house," Lucy said softly.

Very slowly she walked to the base of the attic stairs and just stood there. She started to shake uncontrollably. Suddenly, the home's history leapt into her mind. One of the neighbors had told of the frequent quarrel between Jacob and June about the hated still. "June," she whispered, "if that you stomping your foot and scaring me for nothing, I'll kill you even if you're already dead."

Knock – Knock – Knock

She closed her eyes for a few seconds and gritted her teeth before confronting a thief or a ghost. Slowly, carefully, stepping over the one step that always squeaked, she walked up the stairs. Part way up she stopped to wipe her sweating hands on her pants. She was alone with no way to summon help, but her outrage pushed her forward. This was her home now; June had better shut up if it was her and if it was a robber, he would certainly not be leaving with any of their possessions.

She paused just outside the attic door.

Knock – Knock – Knock

She tucked the flashlight tightly under her left arm pit, put her left hand on the door knob, and raised her right hand with the pop-can weapon high above her head in a threatening manner. Drawing three deep breathes, then holding the fourth breath, she slowly, quietly turned the door knob. Hesitating for only a couple of seconds she kicked the door wide with her right foot and then and then…

Lucy slumped to her knees and cried with relief. Her husband's old wooden baseball bat was rolling against the door. Lucy sat on the floor in the doorway and cried and laughed all at once.

She looked at her right hand and then laughed hysterically out loud. "Now just what good is a can of pop going to do?" she proclaimed aloud. "That would have stopped someone. Well, June, I'd have been better off to follow your lead- an axe would have been much better." Lucy convulsed so hard in laughter again that she lay on the attic floor as tears of mirth streamed down her face.

She carried the bat downstairs and propped it against the fireplace. "Might be a bit more effective that a can," she said.

The next morning Lucy's husband walked into the family room carrying a bag of donuts. "Sorry about last night," he said and noticed the baseball bat leaning against the hearth. "Boy, does that bring back the memories! I loved that old bat. What made you bring that down here?"

Lucy just shrugged and smiled. It took her a few years to confess to arming herself with a can of pop to confront an intruder or the home's resident angry ghost.

15. The Hero Light

When I mentioned to a friend that one of my favorite places is Sevier County, Tennessee, she asked if I knew the story of the light in the woods. Oh boy! A strange light in the woods! Nothing could be better! We headed for the nearest restaurant, set down with coffee, and she told me the old tale. The following is her story.

Sevier County is home to the entrance to the Great Smoky Mountains National Park, the most beautiful country I have ever seen. The hills, the wildlife and the clear flowing streams are lovely beyond description.

Many of these forests have been untouched for years and years. The Cherokee Indians lived in these hills until the white man came and things soon began to change. Businesses such as saw mills, general stores, and taverns sprung up through out the territory. Regardless of who was already living there, settlers claimed the land as their own land and quickly began building cabins, corrals, and barns.

Fortunately for those of us living today, some places have been left as untouched wilderness. There are numerous tracts of virgin timber that are only accessible by foot.

In Sevier County there is one small, densely wooded area that has never been developed. No one is exactly sure why this section of ground has been left untouched. Over the past countless years hunters have walked the floor of these woods and hikers have explored the area looking for wildflowers, birds, or just taking pleasure in the novelty of pristine wilderness.

For years, people have noticed a soft light that rises up during the nighttime hours from one particular location in the woods. The light emits a soft yellow glow, much like a harvest moon in the fall. The light floats slowly around the forest paths and then returns to its original location.

Few folks who live near the old woods venture in during the nighttime and always warn their children to stay away from that wooded area. No one has ever reported being harmed but many describe a sense of danger that permeates the forest at night. It is just understood that people only explore into the woodland during the day and, then, usually in pairs; but never, never during the night.

The brave few that have risked the adventure describe a round light moving through the trees as if following a path. It progressed at a leisurely walking pace. However, if the person watching the light takes a step closer to it, the light freezes and does not move again until they retreat.

The light is always a soft yellow glow, not a bright beam. Locals speculate that the source may be the ghost of an Indian who was buried in the woods where he wanders at night looking for members of his tribe or maybe trying to find his way home.

A few years ago a family moved into Sevier County from Western Tennessee. They were thrilled to find a house with acreage that was still close to the city for shopping and work. The children had room to play and space to raise animals for their 4-H projects.

Six year Mark was the youngest in the family. Late one sunny Saturday afternoon about four weeks after moving to the area, Mark wandered away from his new house.

Apparently, the woods had become inviting and little Mark wanted to do some exploring on his own.

He pretended to be a great hunter, stalking game to shoot for fur and meat. He had heard his uncles talking about their adventures. He stole into the dense woods, imitating what he pictured as them tracking big game through the untamed land.

When Mark did not come home for supper, his parents and siblings began walking around the neighborhood looking for him. They traveled in all directions up and down the roadway with their neighbors soon joining the hunt. Though father kept calling, "Mark, Mark, where are you?" there was no answer and the boy didn't turn up. As night approached, his father called the sheriff. Several deputies joined the search and widened the grid to include the woods.

As darkness descended, so did the temperatures. Fear rippled through the crew who now feared for the boy's safety. Close to midnight, one of the men noticed a ball of soft, yellow light floating about twenty feet above the trees. Hushed murmurs passed between the searchers. Many had witnessed that glow floating along the forest's trails before, but this light was much brighter and larger that the legend described. And, instead of wandering the paths, this light was completely stationary.

Mesmerized, a couple of the men started walking towards the light when a deputy called out "Hey fellas, stop! We don't have time to ghost hunt tonight. Besides, you know that if you get too close the light will move and fade away."

On replied, "Look, the light's a lot brighter than normal. We need to check it out."

The deputy said, "Wait a second. I'm going to call the chief and ask him to send over a few more men, just in case of trouble."

He talked into his cell and after a short discussion he agreed. "Be careful, Joe and take a couple of guys with you," the chief said. "I'll be there in five minutes with some back up."

Two men, including the father, volunteered. The deputy took the lead as the trio was swallowed up by the dense trees. With a flashlight in one hand and the other hand resting on the butt of his pistol, the deputy led his suddenly quiet posse into the woods, swinging his flashlight back and forth across the barely visible path.

Due to the dense woods and the undergrowth of shrub-like vegetation, the men walked single file in a twisted pattern, stepping carefully to avoid fallen branches and large rocks. Finally they neared the location with the light high above them. No one spoke a word. The deputy now had his gun drawn. The volunteers stood about four feet behind him, anxiously sifting from one foot to the other.

The closer they came to the light, the higher and higher it rose until it was about thirty feet above the ground. Lying at the bottom of a circle of soft light was a little boy; fast asleep on his right side atop a small mound of pine needles and leaves.

His father pushed the deputy aside and quickly scooped his son up into his arms, crushing him against his chest. Mark quickly woke up and asked, "Where is the nice man?"

"What man? Who are you talking about?" his father asked.

The other men turned and looked about them but saw no one. They turned quietly back to the young boy and strained to hear what he was saying.

Finally, the deputy interrupted. "What are you talking about, son? I don't see anybody." He swung the flashlight in a large arch to prove his point.

"The nice man was here right here. He made me a bed of leaves and promised to stay beside me until you came."

"What did he look like?" the deputy asked.

"He was dressed like an Indian, but he wasn't scary. He had really neat brown leather pants and moccasins. Can I get some moccasins? Huh, Daddy? Can I? Can I?" Quiet laughter rippled through the group that looked upward as the ball of light started to fade.

His father believed that the spirit of an Indian had protected his son. The other men didn't know what to think. They slapped each other on the back and headed home, happy that the boy had been found unharmed.

"That kid's got some imagination," the deputy murmured.

"Maybe," replied the father. "These old woods keep secrets we can't explain. My son knows what he saw."

What he didn't share with his friends was that the light had stirred a memory that lay deep within him. Though many generations removed, there was Cherokee blood running through his veins and also those of his son. He believed that the spirit of his ancestor and heard his plea and answered it by protecting his son. The very next night, he crept into the suddenly friendly forest and lit a small campfire at the exact spot where they'd found Mark. He sat on the ground and watched the embers float toward the sky like fire flies.

"Thank you, Ancestor. Tonight I honor you by bringing the light."

16.   The Fisherman

Where ever there is a river surrounded by mountains and woods, legends and stories flourish like trout. This story takes place in beautiful Eastern Kentucky. However, I will not name this particular river because I know the area depends on fishermen and boaters to support the local economy.

The river has been a favorite of serious fishermen for years and years. Locals have always enjoyed its fresh fish, and in recent years, city folk have come from several states to vacation in the beauty of the area and enjoy the wonderful fishing even more than those who live nearby.

The river twists and turns. It is lined with huge boulders and sports manageable white water. Canoeists love the challenge of the river; the rapids are quick and noisy, but easy to maneuver as the sudden twists give way to stretches of straight smooth water only to be replaced again by large rocks jutting from the surface.

Though the river is ideal for many forms of recreation, swimming is not one of them. The strong current, the sudden and deep drop-offs in the river bed, and the underwater rocks can make it deadly. Sadly, many cannot seem to resist.

Years ago, a warm summer night with a full moon were just too tempting for a couple of teens looking for adventure and a little rebellion. Buddy and Sarah found a secluded spot down a dirt road that led to the river. After helping themselves to the ice cold beer in the cooler they'd hidden in the trunk, they waded into the shallows of the river's edge.

"C'mon, Sarah," Buddy said as he whipped his tee shirt over his head and threw it into the bushes on the bank, "It's a perfect night for a swim."

"You're on," she said as she followed suit and submerged to her neck in a fit of giggles.

With the car radio blaring rock and roll carried across the river, they paddled into the calm water, lost in the thrill of the evening. Sarah was swimming in a lazy circle floating on her back. Buddy swam further and further into the river, calling out to his girlfriend, "Watch this!"

Sarah answered, "Check out this moon. It's amazing."

Suddenly, a scream of terror pierced the placid night. Sarah flipped over and paddled desperately toward a pair of arms waving madly in the air before they disappeared beneath the black water.

"Buddy! Buddy!" her cries echoed against the rocks as the strength of the current sent terror coursing through her body. She frantically swam for the shore. "I'll get help! Hold on, Buddy!" She grabbed her shirt and pulled it over her head as she ran clumsily through the bush toward the car. With shaking hands, she turned the keys dangling from the ignition and threw dirt in all directions as she raced over the road for home.

Sarah ran through the front door of her home and finally sputtered the details of Buddy sinking from sight amidst heaving sobs. They called Buddy's parents and then called the local sheriff and herded their daughter back to the car to help pinpoint the location where they'd begun the ill-fated swim.

By the time Sarah had led the search party to where Buddy's shirt remained dangling from a bush, clouds had covered the moon. The only light came from flashlights criss-crossing the brush as the rescuers stumbled over the uneven land, finding nothing. Searching the ever changing water in the complete darkness was out of the question. Reluctantly, the deputies abandoned the search until morning.

At first light the searchers returned and combed the river banks again while divers did their best to probe the fast moving water. For several days they looked and looked, watched by Sarah and her friends from the road.

A week later, Buddy's body was found several miles downstream, wedged against large rocks. The tragedy of his drowning was repeated in all the households near the river about how a decision to ignore the dangers could change an adventure into disaster in the blink of an eye.

Time passed with no further incidents of drowning in that river. People moved away and new folks moved into the area and the story of Buddy's death faded from memory, though teens who sneaked to the river's edge under the cover of night still whispered about seeing arms waving from the stream, followed by a girl's high-pitched scream.

Then, history took a new, though equally deadly turn for a visitor from Cincinnati, Ohio. Carl had been fishing for about four years and thought that what he lacked in experience, he made up for by reading everything he could get his hands on concerning sport fishing.

He stopped at the local bait shop for supplies. While the owner rambled on about the dangers of the river and fishing techniques, Carl interjected, "I've done a lot of research on this stream. Besides, my casting techniques are just as good as the good old boys I've watched on ESPN. I don't think paying for a local guide would improve my catch, though it would certainly lighten my wallet."

As Carl walked confidently from his store, the shop owner just shook his head and murmured in disgust, "City people!"

Carl drove his fancy new Jeep out to the river's edge and pulled on his new waders. It was early morning and he was alone. He paused at the bank with his state-of-the-art reel over his shoulder, taking in the sound of the rapids roaring in the distance and day-dreamed of lounging by the pool back at the motel as he emailed fish stories back to the office while sipping a cold one.

With a determined step, he waded into the cold, strong flowing water. *This is the life*, he thought. He cast and cast again. Within a half hour, he had a couple good size trout to show for his efforts. He'd been right. Four years of practice and a whole lot of research were all that fishing required. Full of confidence, he decided that his third catch might be the biggest yet.

He took one more step toward deeper water and suddenly everything went black. As the water took him under, he thought, 'Man, this can't be happening!' His prize pole was forgotten as his arms failed wildly, fighting to surface through the water which pulled him deeper and deeper into its' depths. As his waders filled with water, the added weight made his descent even faster.

A couple of days later, the abandon Jeep was found parked at the river bank but Carl was nowhere to be found. The authorities searched for a couple of weeks but all that was ever found were broken pieces of an expensive fishing pole floating down stream.

White water rafting became a popular spring time sport along this section of the river.   Many of the thrill-seekers began reporting something even more unsettling than the boulders and rushing water. In the early morning hours, they saw a face floating beneath an inch of water. The eyes and mouth were wide open in silent terror. The face would linger for a few seconds and disappear.

One day a rafting guide who'd seen the face often returned in the afternoon with a plan. Outfitted with diving gear, he explored beneath the river's surface.

Quickly, he discovered a deep underwater hole. Further and further down he dived, with the light from his flashlight guiding him. At the bottom, he discovered a skull. When he surfaced, he called in the local authorities who recovered the remains of the missing Ohio fisherman who'd refused the aid of someone who really knew this river in favor of research and misplaced confidence.

When the man's body was returned for burial, the face was never seen again. Locals speculated that he just wanted to go back to Ohio where his life had been safer.

As for the rafting guide, he continued to take vacationers down the river for years to come, telling the story of the ghostly face beneath the water that belonged to a city slicker that didn't have the sense to pay for a guide.

17. Lover's Leap

Every county seems to have a Lover's Leap. Washington County, Ohio is no different. Here is one more story of two young lovers with a tragic ending.

By 1880, the territory along the Ohio River was well established. Plentiful land with beautiful rolling hills that were the end of the Appalachian Mountains was a magnet for settlers and businesses. Thanks to the river, new communities could trade with cities to the west and south as far as the Gulf of Mexico.

A strong work ethic was already in place in the county when young Samuel moved there with his family from the Carolinas. His father set up a saw mill near the river to provide lumber for continuous construction of homes and businesses as well as for boat builders.

Samuel's father thought that a strong back and hard work were the most important things in life. Nothing else mattered to him except making money. The only education he needed was enough mathematics to count his receipts and keep track of who owed the mill money!

About the same time, Sarah and her family moved from the east coast in Virginia so that her father, Benjamin, could start his practice as a physician. They had long wanted to escape the hot, humid Virginia summers and her father believed the need for physicians in the developing country was a terrific opportunity for his young family.

Family, faith and serious education were important to Sarah's father. They were very close and she was his pride and joy. Shortly after their arrival in Ohio, her mother died from a severe case of influenza and young Sarah was all that her father had.

Benjamin helped Sarah with the house work as much as he could, so that she could spend time with her friends and enjoy being a young girl. He knew that soon enough she would have her own household to care for.

Sarah was faithful in her school attendance and took pride in earning good grades. She often helped the teacher with the younger children, enjoying the progress they made in reading and writing. Soon, she was dreaming of teaching in her own classroom.

Samuel, on the other hand, was able to attend school only when the mill was not running or his father gave him a rare day off from work. Though his mother fought hard for Samuel's education, the bulk of his instruction came from his mother's efforts after the work day was done. Since his father was quite successful without any formal schooling, he just did not understand the value of an education. This was always a source of contention between the two parents, causing many harsh words to be exchanged.

Samuel and Sarah met at school where a childhood friendship developed into much more. By sixteen, they were head-over-heels in love and daydreaming of a wedding. While marriage at this age was not unusual in this era, there was a problem. Samuel's father was in favor of the marriage, thinking it would motivate Samuel to work full time at the mill and forget about this school nonsense. The responsibility of supporting a family who needed an income would secure an heir for the business that he'd built.

Sarah's father wanted his daughter to graduate from high school and then obtain her teaching certificate. He also wanted Sarah to continue to live at home with him, for at least a few more years. She looked so much like her mother that it eased the pain of Benjamin's loss. He dreaded being left alone and loosing this last link to his deceased wife.

The teenagers saw no easy solution to their problem. After several months of trying to please everyone, the young couple decided they had no choice but to run away and start their lives together far from the well-meaning, but unacceptable needs of their families.

Over a period of several weeks the lovers hid one needed item at a time in a secret cave. Samuel often reminded Sarah to "Bring only things that we can carry. A wagon would slow down our progress and make us easy to find."

When the couple decided that they had accumulated everything they needed, they set a somewhat flexible departure date. Every item was carefully packed and tested for weight. Sarah had even managed to hide a small amount of money. They hoped for a rainy day that would stop the mill's operation, providing Samuel with a rare day off work.

And, if the day was a Wednesday, that would work perfectly because Sarah always spent that morning in town shopping. Neither would be missed for several hours, giving them a head start.

When a rainy Wednesday finally arrived, they stole away to their special cave to gather their stored provisions. Within a half hour they had everything packed. Holding hands and smiling into each other's loving eyes, they began their journey toward a new life together.

Before long, the rain stopped and the sun was dazzling in a clear blue sky. Samuel suggested that they hike to the lookout and get a final view of the big Ohio River and the town where they'd first met. Sarah agreed and soon the couple reached the lookout where they'd often spent stolen moments together.

In her eagerness to have one final look at the river below and the home she shared with her father, Sarah stepped too close to the edge of the mountain side. On the muddy ground still wet from the rain, her feet slipped out from under her and she fell, sliding, and rolling head over heels, down the cliffs.

Her screams reverberated against the hills and were suddenly quiet as she landed against a large out cropping of rock.

Horrified, Samuel slid down the treacherous mountain with tears streaming from his eyes. He found her lifeless body lying against the rocks and cradled her to his breast. He just rocked back and forth for several minutes. His Sarah was gone forever.

What should he do? Would people believe it was an accident? Would Sarah's father blame him for her death? How could he face Benjamin?

In a panic, Samuel made a fast decision. He laid Sarah on the ground next to the rocks were she died and covered her with clothing from her pack. Then he placed small rocks over her to make a crude grave.

Samuel gathered up his pack and took off, never returning to the area. He headed west and then south to the Ohio River where he found a ride on a river boat and ended up in far, western Kentucky where he blended in as just another young man in search of a new life.

Years later, Sarah's remains were found and she was given a proper burial in the town cemetery and the gossip swirled. Had Sarah fallen or was she pushed? And just where was Samuel?

"They were sweethearts, you know," said a neighbor lady one day at the store. "Her father never approved, so she must have taken her own life and the poor boy disappeared, unable to cope with his grief."

But others had different opinions. "Something strange happened up on that mountain, and that boy ran to avoid the law!"

"There is no way he'd harm her. They were in love, like Romeo and Juliet."

"Guess we'll never know for sure. You never really know a person, do you?" And so it went.

Samuel was never heard from again. After a while, idle chat about the location that was now called, 'Lover's Leap,' became more myth than fact. In fact, visitors to the overlook often talked of seeing the misty figure of a young girl standing at the cliff's edge who suddenly disappears. Many come to the spot, hoping for a glimpse of the 'ghost' while others avoid that particular location, not wanting to slip to their deaths as they believed Sarah had.

In recent years, a successful photographer decided to climb the mountain to take pictures of the spectacular view of the Ohio River, hoping to turn them into a calendar.

When he returned from his shoot, his assistant asked how it had gone.

The photographer replied, "I took plenty of pictures because the river was swarming with boats and light on the hills was breath taking. But an overwhelming sense of sadness – or maybe fatigue - came over me so I decided to pack it in for the day."

His assistant, a local who knew the history of the lookout, just smiled and told him the story of 'Lover's Leap.'

"C'mon, this is the twenty-first century and you're still talking about a Lover's Leap, complete with a resident ghost.

How quaint!" he laughed. "I'm bushed. See you in the morning."

The next day his assistant hovered over his shoulder as he downloaded the images from his camera. There were many shots of the scenery, so he quickly saved and deleted his way through the hundreds of images. He was about to delete one that showed the trail leading to the top of the cliff when he suddenly leaned so close to the computer screen that his nose was nearly touching it. At the top of the ridge was the faint outline of a young girl looking out over the river in the exact spot where he'd taken so many pictures. But he'd spent hours alone on that mountain top, not even seeing someone on his way back down.

His assistant just laughed and patted his shoulder. "Yep, that's Sarah. I told you so. So, who's quaint now?"

Mountain Spirits

18.   The Tree

This is a tale from Eastern Tennessee that has been shared for generations. Is it true? No one knows for sure.

"May! May!" someone called.

"Did you hear that, Mom?" eighteen year old Cathy asked her mother as they walked along the road to their farm.

"Yes dear, I heard it loud and clear" her mother, Wanda, replied.

Cathy's family had lived in these mountains for years and she loved the stories about her family settling on the old homestead. The history of the mountains and the hardships of settling the territory fascinated her. In fact, Cathy thought that someday she just might write a book about the legends and folklore of the area.

Mountain Spirits

The year was 1932 and Cathy had graduated from school one month ago. Cathy and her boyfriend planned to be married that fall after the harvest was completed.

As Cathy and Wanda walked home from the general store with the few supplies that they could afford, they both heard the shouting of "May! May!" again. Both women stopped in their tracks and looked at each other with questioning faces.

Wanda shook her head. "I don't recall those cries ever being that loud."

Cathy asked, "Is that the story about the young lovers?" Wanda nodded. "Oh, please, Mom, tell the story again. I haven't heard it in years."

In the early 1800's, when this area was just being settled, the woods were thick with tall spreading trees. Oak, walnut, hickory, and maple trees were are all in abundant supply, just perfect for building a home. But if you wished to homestead, the land had to first be cleared of rocks and trees.

Young George and his bride Elizabeth had purchased a piece of fertile land in the valley. Georges' nickname for his wife was May, in honor of the month in which they were married.

The newly-weds dreamed of starting their marriage in their own cabin on their own land. That meant that they had to clear a small patch of the thick trees for the cabin as well as the lean-to shelter and corral for the animals that they intended to raise, and, eventually, a barn. But, first things first. They marked the ground where they'd begin with the cabin and set to work.

Elizabeth watched George every day as he chopped down the necessary trees. Together they cut off the branches and stacked everything so the wood could dry and the building could soon begin. It was back-breaking work, but they were together.

When George paused in the never-ending labor, he frequently found Elizabeth gazing at him with loving eyes and his exhaustion vanished, replaced by pride in providing the beginning of their new life. He also watched in amazement as Elizabeth worked tirelessly next to him trimming off the branches and carrying the wood.

"Now Elizabeth, you be careful. I don't want you to over do," George told her daily. But deep inside George knew that he could never have done this building all by himself and was both proud and grateful that his wife was as dedicated to their home as he was.

George was always careful to make sure that Elizabeth was not in the way of a falling tree. By working together, the young couple soon had plenty of trees cut to begin their cabin in the space they'd marked.

George decided to cut an oak tree to use for building some furniture for their new home. This 'special' tree would be set aside for drying.

Telling Elizabeth to stand to the south he made the final cuts to the large oak tree. He looked at Elizabeth with a huge smile and then swung the axe one last time, knowing that this cut would send the tree falling to the ground. As the tree groaned to begin its' fall, a strong gust of wind swept through the valley causing the tree to fall towards Elizabeth.

"Look out!" yelled George in horror, as Elizabeth lurched to the side.

"Oh my god – oh my god," George screamed as he raced toward her. Elizabeth lay on the ground with a bloody scrape on her head where one of the tree's branches had grazed her, knocking her to the ground. He fell to his knees, wrapped his arms around her and lifted her gently from the ground. Beneath her head was a blood-soaked rock.

George could not believe it! He was always so careful to protect his precious Elizabeth.

With shaking hands, George hitched the horse to the wagon as quickly as possible, and then he gathered Elizabeth into his arms and placed her gently in the back, covering her with blankets.

He raced down the road toward the small nearby settlement hoping that someone would have some medical knowledge to help him. "I'll get you some help, May. I'll get you some help!" he repeated over and over as he drove the horses on, the wagon bumping wildly over the rough terrain.

Halfway there, he stopped the wagon to check on his Elizabeth. Looking at his beloved and knew the truth: the eyes in her pale face, no longer smiled up at him with profound devotion. Elizabeth was dead. His precious Elizabeth was gone forever.

George slumped to his knees, staring at the ground. "May, oh May, what will I do?" he cried.

Taking a deep breath, George stood up and reached under the wagon seat for his rifle. He looked one last time at his wife, placed the barrel of the rifle under his chin and pulled the trigger. A minute later, George rejoined his bride.

~

Cathy and her mother had reached their home by the end of the story and dropped down to sit on the porch steps. "How sad," Cathy sighed as she leaned against the porch railing. After several minutes of silence, she continued. "You never know how life will turn out, do you, Mom?" Cathy said.

"No, Honey, you don't," Wanda replied. Picking up the thread of the story, she continued. "You know, some folks tell of hearing the sound of a wagon racing down the road but not seeing anything. I never have, but I do hear that pitiful voice yelling for May. I've never seen anyone, but, the sound of those cries just breaks my heart."

Both ladies just sat there for a few minutes with neither one talking. "You know, Mom, every time I walk past that old abandoned cabin down the road, I feel so sad. Do you suppose that was where George and May lived?"

"Oh, I don't know, Cathy. I feel a bit sad, myself, but it makes me smile to think that they loved each other that much. Just like I hope that you and your husband will someday."

To this day, people in this part of the state still hear the screams of "May! May!" and the sounds of a ghost wagon racing down the old winding road. No one is ever afraid. In fact, they think of it as a reminder of how short life can be, and, for some reason, rush home to hug their loved ones.

Mountain Spirits

19.   The Soldier

Some wars and battles never end. This story is about a Confederate soldier who is still ready to defend his home state of Kentucky.

Vicky lived alone in the old farm house that had been in her family for over one hundred years. Her husband of thirty years had passed away following a long illness. Her children were grown and had their own homes near by. How lucky she felt to have family close with her roots firmly planted.

Vicky loved that old house and its family history and knew that she would never leave it. The old place was a part of her. She found comfort in the family photos scattered about, the furniture, some of which had been in the family for years, and the old trees, which had been planted by her ancestors, that provided shade for the house and yard. This was home. This was *her* home.

To keep busy, and also to earn some money, Vicky worked at a local grocery store. It was a small shop and she worked the night shift, which suited her fine. She enjoyed the nocturnal pace of the store when most of her neighbors were sleeping.

She stocked the shelves and waited on the few customers who shopped then, and always kept a coffee pot brewing. One of her few regulars was the night patrolman. Vicky made him a nightly sandwich from the delicatessen and refilled the black coffee in his mug while they chatted to fill the silence before returning to their respective jobs.

After work, Vicky went home every morning, had a bowl of cereal and went to bed in the upstairs bedroom; her favorite room in the house. It was situated in a corner with windows on two sides of the house that always provided a gentle breeze.

From one window she could look at the wooded mountain side. The other window gave her a view of the garden and the small creek that flowed through the property. Every morning, Vicky would count her blessings before drifting off to sleep in the cool air.

Rita Arnold

As a child, Vicky heard stories about the Confederate soldiers from her area that fought in the 'War.' Their graves were clearly marked in the local cemetery and were respectfully tended by the citizens. Every solder's grave was plainly marked with a bronze plaque and on Memorial Day, a new small American flag was placed by the headstone.

In fact, Vicky's Great Grandfather had fought in the 'War of Northern Aggression', a fact her Grandmother often spoke of proudly. Her Granny talked as if the South should have won the war and did not understand why they had surrendered. Though Vicky found all this interesting, she felt as if her Grandmother was becoming confused in her older years, talking so much about the distant past.

Vicki felt she was overdue to visit her husband's grave, but it was hard to make the trip to the cemetery. Sometimes the memories of happier times with her husband would weigh on her, so she put it off. However, it had been several weeks since her last trip and her sense of duty kept her absence on her mind. Since it was in the same cemetery, she vowed to visit her Great Grandfather's grave as well. These thoughts were floating through her mind as she lay down to rest after her shift at the store. Someday, she would absolutely make that trip, but today she was too tired.

Normally Vicky slept through the day never waking until the afternoon when she would arise to eat and get ready for work. But today was different. About mid-morning something woke her and she absently looked outside. She could not believe what she saw.

Beneath one of the trees that shaded the yard was a Confederate soldier, standing at attention and looking straight at her. She rubbed her eyes and looked again. Yes, he was still there. He looked so very young, no more than a teenager. She stared at him for some minutes before he began to fade away. "N*ow what was that all about,*" she wondered.

Had she been dreaming? Were there re-enactors in the area? Surely, she would have heard something at the store if a reenactment had been planned in the community?

Vicky lay back down but sleep would not return. She reminisced about the stories her Grandmother had told over the years as she willed herself back to sleep. Suddenly Vicky sat up in bed, remembering the tale! Could the old story have been true?

During the Civil War, a small band of Confederate soldiers had camped for a few days behind the family barn while waiting for the rest of their regiment to join them. One of the young soldiers, eager for battle, was always seen walking around in his new uniform. He practiced standing guard thinking it would help prepare him for the battle with the ….Yankees.

But one rainy spring day the young soldier caught a fever. Nothing the doctors did for the youngster could bring down his temperature. Soon, in his delirium, the boy was calling for his mother. A day later he passed away and was buried in the town cemetery.

Vicky's Grandmother told her that the boy only appeared to women and only during the spring. Could the young Confederate standing on her lawn have been him?

Unable to sleep, Vicky got dressed and drove to the cemetery. She visited the graves of her husband and Great-grandfather, placed flowers from her garden on their graves and then found the headstone of the young soldier in her Grandmother's tale. She promised herself that she would return in a few days with flowers for him.

For the many years of her long life, Vicky saw the vision of the young Confederate soldier every spring, feeling that he was lonely and needed some company. And, each spring, she picked flowers from her garden not only for the relatives that rested in the nearby cemetery, but for the young man who visited her home each year.

Vicky's daughter taught American History at the local high school. She was the only person that Vicky had told about the Confederate soldier's annual visits. The daughter was deeply touched by her mother's caring for the forgotten grave.

"Promise me that when I'm gone, you'll bring flowers every year; not just to the family, but to that boy as well. Everyone deserves to be remembered."

Several years later Vicky died in her sleep. Her daughter's family moved into the old family home that Vicky had loved. And every spring, her daughter kept her promise to

Vicky. Of course, it helped that each year in the springtime morning hours she looked from her window to find a Confederate soldier standing at attention under the branches of the old maple, staring straight into her eyes.

Mountain Spirits

20.   The Brother

The following is a story that was shared with me as a legend or folklore that has been told for years and years. No one knows if there is any truth to it, but the story survives. It is your decision to believe it or not, but the legends of rural America that evolved over the years are wonderful and need to be preserved.

In 1948, twenty-four year old Olivia had just graduated from college and was fulfilling her dream of returning home to her beloved wooded hills by the Ohio River. She was going to teach fourth grade among her family and friends where she could hike and camp and fish. God, how she'd missed fishing when she had worked toward her degree. Her dream was about to come true.

She had worked several jobs to pay for her college education and now she planned to help her students learn the value of hard work. She had gone to college and loved studying and learning, but she wasn't rich, so she had worked and worked hard to put herself through school. She slaved away at night shifts as a waitress, spent week-ends clerking in the grocery store, and even managed a few hours of restocking the shelves in the college library. But she kept plugging away. She had a goal: one day she'd go home, but this time as a teacher.

Olivia missed the rolling hills, the thick forested woodlands and the beauty of the changing seasons that surrounded her home. Near by was the ever-flowing mighty Ohio River with its boats and barges called to her of the heritage of those early days.

During the few hours of sleep she managed during her college years, she dreamed of driving down the old country roads of her home in her decrepit old car. The only strange part of that dream was the unidentified man who sat beside her. "Who was he?" she often asked herself as she awoke.

He seemed to be a few years older than she and reminded her of her father when he was younger. She was never afraid of her passenger. He merely sat there, watched the passing scenery and slowly turned his head to smile at her as they drove along the twisting highway. He never spoke a single word, but he was always smiling. Who could he be?

Throughout her first year of teaching, she still had this recurring dream of driving through the countryside with the man sitting beside her. Still, she had no idea who he was. She never mentioned her dream to anyone for fear people would think that she was crazy!

Olivia lived in a small house about ten miles south of the school along a winding road lined with trees. An old steel bridge crossed a strong flowing stream on that drive, which somehow reminded her of the dream and her unidentified passenger.

One spring morning before work, Olivia listened to the rain beating on the metal roof of her house. She wondered if flooding was a possibility today. The area had just finished a winter with the largest amount of snow fall in recorded history. The heavy rains, combined with the run off of the melting snow threatened to push the swollen creeks and streams over the tops of their banks.

Olivia was aware that flooding could occur at any moment and she needed to allow extra time in driving to school. She wasn't afraid because she had grown up around here and knew every roadway. But she was smart enough to know that she must be careful.

With her boots on and raincoat wrapped tightly around her, Olivia raced outside to her car. Praying that the old car would start, she turned the key in the ignition and smiled as the engine came to life. She allowed her aging vehicle a few minutes to warm up, made sure the wiper blades were working and started out on her drive.

The rain was coming down in torrents and Olivia could only see a few feet in front of her. She took each curve slowly and moved at a snail's pace in the straight-aways. She had such a tight grip on the steering wheel that her knuckles were turning white and her hands were starting to cramp. Her neck and shoulders ached from the tension of hunching over the steering wheel.

The lightning flashed across the sky followed by a loud crack. BANG! BANG! Each strobe of white light made her jump in her seat, followed by thunder that roared for several seconds. BOOM! BOOM! BOOM! It was so loud the car seemed to rock on its tires.

Suddenly the inside of her car was white from lightning striking very near her car. She looked in the rearview mirror and watched a tree fall across the road behind her. *"Whew! – that was close,"* she thought. Now she knew that she could not turn back and must continue on to the school.

With another deafening bang, a second tree fell across the road, this time ahead of her. She stomped on the brake and stopped the car, not sure what to do next. Two trees had fallen; one in front and the other behind her. The old road was too narrow for her to turn the car around, but even if she could, both directions were blocked.

The wipers were at full speed trying to keep up with the rain while she searched for the answer of what to do next. For several minutes Olivia just sat there, staring at the rain drops on the windshield. *"Think,"* she told herself. *"You're educated, now think,"* she said softly.

Not only was she trapped between two fallen trees, she was fairly sure that the bridge up ahead was probably washed out as well. Walking in this weather was impossible. She wanted to cry but knew that would not solve her dilemma either.

Olivia looked to her right and there sat the man who had been in her dreams for years and years. Even now, wide awake, she was still not afraid. She said. "Who are you? What should I do?"

"Drive on" the man replied.

"What?" she nearly screamed. "Are you crazy?"

"Drive on. Up ahead is a seldom used old logging road, turn left there" he answered. He smiled at her and then turned to look at the road.

She sat still for a couple of indecisive minutes and then slowly, gripping the steering wheel even tighter with the wiper blades throwing the rain from her windshield as fast as they could, she inched the car forward. Olivia wiped the moisture from the inside of the windshield with a hankie but still it was difficult to see more than a few feet ahead.

"So far, so good. Are you sure there is no other way out of here? And just who are you?"

He just smiled a friendly smile and said, "I'm sure. You're a good driver. I've watched you for years."

Slowly, carefully, she turned onto the dirt road. After only a short distance, she stopped in front of a rickety, old wooden bridge. She turned toward her passenger and said in her firm teacher's voice, "You've got to be kidding if you think I'm driving across that old bridge!"

He just smiled and pointed to the bridge. After a few minutes she continued on and safely crossed the bridge. Eventually, she made it back onto the main road and stopped to take a few slow, deep breathes to relax her breathing and to calm the beating in her chest.

She looked over at the man and said, "Tell me who you are. Why are you in my car? Explain yourself or else I'm driving straight to the sheriff's office."

Again, he smiled. "I'm your older brother. I've always looked out for you."

"What!" she gasped. Olivia felt a chill run through her and in a soft whisper said, "I don't have any brothers."

"Sure, you do," he replied. "You see, our mother miscarried a few years before you were born. She was so devastated that she and our father agreed to never mention it to anyone. They just could not bear to talk about my passing."

"It's yours! The marker in the family plot in the cemetery, the marker with no writing, next to Grandfather's belongs to you." Olivia shouted.

The man nodded. "Yep, that one's for me."

There was so much she wanted to ask but as the rain stopped, her brother smiled and quickly disappeared. She smiled all the way to school, knowing that her very own guardian angel would be there no matter what storm she passed through.

21. The Fight for Love

The following is an old legend that has been told for many years in Eastern Tennessee. I hope and pray that it is only folklore and not a true story.

"Mom! Mom!" Connie called out as she raced into the back door. "I just saw the ghost lady running in the pasture!" said Connie. Her mother gave Connie a few minutes to catch her breath and then told her sit down. "What did she look like?" her mother asked. Connie perfectly described Rachel.

"Connie, honey, I want to tell you a story about that pasture. Perhaps it's just a story so maybe it's true or maybe it's not. Sometimes we see things that can't be explained; that's why they are maybes" her mother said.

~

From the day that Robert was born he always had a special aura about him. His interest in books began at a very young age. He knew his alphabet and could spell some words before he started first grade which was most unusual in the days before Sesame Street. He read everything he could get his hands on. In fact, one of the few books available to him was the Bible which he read from cover to cover several times.

As a student, Robert always received straight A's, and school work came easily to him. Even so, he wasn't cocky or conceited about his grades. He shared his enthusiasm with the younger kids and helped them with their studies.

When Robert was starting the sixth grade a new boy named Tad began coming to his school. After losing his family in a fire up north in Ohio, Tad moved to Eastern Tennessee to live with his aunt and uncle. Tad also earned straight A's but learning was not easy for him. He studied hard every night to prepare for the next day.

Tad craved his aunt and uncle's approval. His secret fear was that if he did not do well in school they would be ashamed of him and send him away to live with some else.

After completing the eighth grade, both sets of parents got together and decided that they should send their exceptionally bright boys to a college prep school in Virginia. The boys, who had become good friends, were thrilled and could hardly wait for the new school year to begin. In the fall Robert and Tad boarded the train and left for the adventure of a new school. They quickly assimilated into their new life, enjoying their studies and making many new friends.

At a school dance Robert met Rachel. She was so beautiful and so much fun that he was smitten. The two of them and Robert's best friend, Tad, were inseparable. Rachel and Tad became really good friends, but Robert and Rachel were special friends, very special friends.

Near the end of their senior year, Robert asked Rachel to marry him and she excitedly answered yes. She looked forward to graduation and the life they would have together.

On the night of the graduation ceremony the boys were out drinking with some friends first time in their lives to celebrate their success. Unused to alcohol, they were soon, talkative and boisterous. Towards the end of the evening, Tad and Robert stumbled back to their room.

Tad stopped and suddenly announced to his friend, "I'm in love with Rachel and want to marry her." Robert's response was to turnaround and punch Tad hard in the jaw sending him crashing to the ground. Tad rubbed his chin as he arose and faced his friend. "We'll settle this tomorrow in the pasture behind the stables. See you at noon unless you haven't got the guts."

Word of the fight spread throughout the school and at noon, several classmates had formed a circle around the boys, taunting them as they warily eyed each other. Neither could back down now, afraid of being called a coward. But secretly neither really wanted to fight his best friend, especially after they awoke with raging hangovers.

Egged on by the jeering crowd, the boys started shoving each other and talking tough for the benefit of their classmates. Before a single punch had been thrown, Rachel ran between them, put a hand on each chest and tried to push them apart while swinging her head back and forth. "Robert! Tad! Stop it! Stop it!"

In their anger, both roughly pushed her arms aside. Rachel was caught off balance, slipped on the damp ground and fell hard against the rocky ground. Robert and Tad looked daggers at each other and waited for her to get up. But Rachel didn't move.

The screaming crowd had fallen silent. Finally someone spoke up. "Shouldn't we do something?" Robert bent down and grabbed the unconscious Rachel under her arms as Tad picked up her feet. They rushed her to the school infirmary where the nurse shoved them from the office and closed the door. An hour later, Rachel had died.

The boys were devastated. They were inconsolable, talking to no one let alone each other. Two days later Tad hung himself from a tree near the pasture and Robert hopped a west bound train, never to be heard from again.

~

"The girl you saw in the pasture, Connie, was Rachel. who is still trying to stop the fight. It seems that when a girl your age is close to graduating, Rachel feels the need to make contact. That's when you see the poor girl running through the pasture that took her life. "

"Why then, Mom?" Connie asked.

Her mother smiled and said "Even old legends can teach important lessons, like acting more mature and not being caught up in a fight. You understand, don't you?"

Connie smiled at her mother and said, "Sure, Mom." To herself she said, *"I understand that boys can be stupid and being caught in the middle of that can really hurt!"*

22.   The Country Church

Everyone should travel through the rural parts of the Appalachians, enjoy the beauty of the mountains and stop to look at the peaceful valleys. Look closely and you'll notice that throughout the countryside nestled among the tall stately trees are small white-painted churches. Most were built on stone foundations as the area was being developed years and years ago. Many are still in use for weekly services, some open only for special occasions, and, sadly, others are not in use at all.

From the 1800's through the early twentieth century, the country church was the focal point of the community. The building often doubled as a one room school house during the week and became a place of prayer and fellowship on Sunday.

In the days before radio, television, or the internet, church activities were usually the main source of social interaction. Church picnics on warm Sunday afternoons, the children's annual Christmas play, and pie raffles to raise funds for the building's maintenance were highly anticipated events among the largely rural communities. Though weddings were usually held in the bride's home, larger affairs also took place in the church, especially if the bride's father was the local pastor.

Drive slowly along one twisting highway in Kentucky and as you round the big curve you might notice a small white clapboard church.

Not only does the building desperately need paint, but the structure is so damaged that it leans slightly to the right. It sits on a crumbling stone foundation made of stones which were gathered from the surrounding property. The number '1842' is scratched into one of the stones at the corner. There are three windows along the east and west sides covered with dirt and cobwebs but the windows are undamaged. The front door sags but you can still push it open on its creaking hinges.

Inside you will find the church filled with bare wooden pews and small wooden pulpit in the front as if waiting for the minister to cross the wide plank floor boards that are now cupping and starting to split.

As the dust dances across the sunbeams that manage to break through the grime of the windows, you can almost hear an old time preacher giving his flock the fire and brimstone message of, "Repent, you sinners. Repent!" Or maybe the preacher this Sunday, he is calmly preaching a message of love and hope with, "Remember, my friends, God loves you and is with you always."

But stop by the church at night and you might see something very different. Park your car a few feet away form the church and quietly walk to the west side of the building. Rub some of the dirt off the pane of the middle window and look inside.

Yes, what you are seeing did actually happen, so just stand still and watch. And do not make a sound.

You might see a radiant bride, dressed in white lace, beaming into the face of her betrothed who stands in full Confederate uniform as they speak their wedding vows! The scene took place in 1862. The War Between the States was raging and the young man dreamt of marching away with his regiment to seek glory for himself and Kentucky and returning triumphantly to the waiting arms of his new wife. What could be more perfect?

As you watch through the window, the newlyweds kiss and turn toward the congregation. But instead of everyone leaving the church with happy smiles or tears of joy, the vision slowly fades away and you hear the sound of wretched sobbing.

Walk a few yards to the north of the church and you will see a small cemetery surrounded by a split rail fence. In the corner closest to the church stands a marker that reads 'Sergeant Billy Bob Arnold, Born 1-28-1841 -- Died 1862, in Virginia in a skirmish with Union soldiers, buried in Virginia.'

To its side is a stone etched with, 'Mrs. Rebecca Arnold, Born, 4-22-1844 -- Died, 9-18-1862.'

Legend has it that Rebecca died of a broken heart when she received the news about her Billy. Immediately after opening the life changing telegram, she took to her bed and never leaving that room again.

The telegram remained in her left hand until the day she died. No one saw her reading the dreadful news again but that telegram was clutched firmly in the same hand that bore her wedding ring, the only thing left of her husband.

Rebecca was buried with the fingers of her left hand still wrapped around the tragic reminder of her shattered life.

There are nights when the moon is blocked by a scattering of clouds and things begin to happen in that cemetery. If you sit quietly across the road without any light source, another surprise may await.

When all chances of daylight are gone, you will see two small round balls of soft light slowly rise up from these two graves. Slowly, slowly, lights rise and hesitate over the markers. They pause side by side for a few minutes and then slowly merge into one brighter ball that drifts upward until it fades into the night sky.

People who have witnessed this event often find gentle tears running down theirs cheeks. As the united light disappears in the sky, they find themselves beaming with happiness because they know that Billy and Rebecca are together - again. Most people return to their cars and silently drive away, deeply moved at what they just witnessed.

Skeptics might say this story is a product of over-active imaginations, but the hopeful believe the scene they've witnessed proves that true love will never die.

This book is filled with stories,
That people say are true,
We'll let the matter of judgment,
Be entirely up to you.

Some ghosts prefer a mountain,
While others choose flat land,
Looking at a mountain daily,
Is something that's really grand.

All ghosts experience emotion,
As with the peaceful dove,
The foundation of our being,
Has to have the presence of love.

The ways of life are many,
Much pleasure is from our giving,
While that's at the top of our list,
We also enjoy country living.

    Milton H. Arnold